SARAH VERNON

The Craft of Crime

First published by Oh Honey Projects 2023

This novel is entirely a work of fiction. The names, characters and incidents portrayed in it are the work of the author's imagination. Any resemblance to actual persons, living or dead, events or localities is entirely coincidental.

Front cover photograph by Alex Jones / Unsplash Images

Back cover photograph by Jess Bailey / Unsplash Images

Title page photograph by Eduardo Casajús Gorostiaga / Unsplash Images

Cover design by Mel D. Truin

www.vernonmysteries.com

First edition

ISBN: 979-8-9873525-3-3

This book was professionally typeset on Reedsy.
Find out more at reedsy.com

Contents

Chapter 1

Like many events, the debacle at Lark Harrier's artist talk had started with a simple request.

"Will you be able to get there early to help us set up?" Martina had asked Monday morning, in the breezily confident manner in which she made most of her requests, as we strode down the hall together after a particularly painful critique session with a student. And as I often did when faced with her self-assured manner, I found myself agreeing before fully considering what helping this particular (and particularly pompous) visiting artist might entail.

"Thank you, Sam, you're an absolute gem!" Martina beamed down at me, before coming to an abrupt halt at the door to the faculty offices. "I'll see you later, thanks again!"

I found myself suddenly alone in the hallway, realizing that I might have been overstepping the bounds of my teaching assistant position just a bit.

Martina St. Aubin had arrived in our art department over the summer, and I had been her teaching assistant for almost as long. The position had been set up by Agnes, another sculpture professor who was solidly my answer for what I wanted to be when I grew up. Martina, likewise, was well on her way to this goal – definitely ahead of me in the looks department, at any rate. Like Agnes, Martina tended to dress in long layers of simply cut dresses and tops, though Martina usually chose bright, saturated colors that matched her equally bright work and provided a vivid contrast to her long dark hair and somewhat severe black-rimmed glasses.

Before our first meeting over the summer, I had looked up Martina's work. Like the course I was assisting her with, she created large assemblages, building them up to create installations that were like movie sets, welcoming you into the unique world of each installation. The first time we met for coffee over the summer, I'm afraid I did a poor job of containing my excitement and (probably puppy-like) admiration. Martina told me she was "interested in exploring hand-driven processes that demonstrate the embodiment of their maker while at the same denying those very people their individuality." I'd nodded sagely. Did I know exactly what she meant by this? No, of course not, and I'd frankly be surprised if anyone did. But did I want her to know this? No, of course not.

Soon, as the semester got started in its usual whirlwind, I was meeting with Martina nearly every day, to go over upcoming assignments and review who said what during the last critique. Martina was also running the visiting artist program this semester, responsible for inviting four visiting artists who would each be with us for up to two weeks. I had dodged any extra duties during the first artist's visit, but didn't get so lucky when it came to Lark.

Lark Harrier had only been at school for one week, and even before the projector episode I could say with confidence that he was a grade A jerk. It was beyond me why Martina had even wanted him on the schedule of visiting artists this semester.

The first artist who'd come, Beverly Marks, was a lovely woman who made intricately carved sculptures depicting various natural phenomena, and who'd delighted everyone with her stories of working in the New York City art world of the '60s and '70s. In contrast, Lark had been a bull in a china shop from day one, when he had practically slaughtered several students in a row in a class critique, and he seemed honestly delighted in making everyone around him miserable. I hate to blame it on his level of success, as I firmly don't believe that there's some kind of secret contract that says every single successful artist must turn into a pompous ass, but it had clearly gone to his head. Lark strode around the building with a mixture of disdain and magnanimousness, as if he were simultaneously taking pity on us and rewarding us just with the very fact of his presence.

He had made his name in the '90s and early 2000s with large scale sculptures in plexiglass and steel, huge contraptions that seemed to defy the laws of physics with their ability to balance and even stand up. I mean, if you asked me, I had kind of assumed this type of sculpture had gone out of style after a huge wave of it in the '70s and '80s, and that people were ready for something new, maybe even representational for once. But I guess not, because Lark had quickly become the star of several major museum shows and seen a simultaneous rise in the prices his sculptures could command. For the past few decades, he had installed as department chair of the sculpture department at a Chicago art school, from which vantage point he had clearly become practiced at reigning over all he saw. Unfortunately for me, everyone had seen my reaction to his reign. On the very same day he died.

By the time I arrived in the auditorium Monday afternoon, it was clear that everyone was already on edge. The gallery assistant, a young woman named Bridget, was hovering on the edge of the room, clearly unsure whether she was meant to intervene in the unfolding drama or stay on the sidelines (which was probably her preference). Martina was standing with Lark in the front of the room near the podium, idly tapping away on her phone while the pair of them waited for another student to get the projector turned on. I called out my hellos from the back of the room, getting a small wave from Martina and a nervous nod from Bridget.

Lark looked over his shoulder at me. "Good," he said. "Are you tech support?"

"I can be!" I said brightly. Years of awful retail jobs over high school summers meant that my customer service charm could still be turned on in a pinch, whether the person throwing a tantrum was an actual child or a middle-aged male artist.

The student working the projector shot me a look that was either exasperated or a warning.

"What seems to be the problem?" I asked.

"The color is completely off. Look at the screen," Lark commanded.

I looked, and saw only the first slide of a pretty typical-looking visiting artist presentation.

"What seems to be the problem?" I asked again.

"The color is completely off," Lark repeated, slowly this time, in case it was my stupidity that was causing the issue.

I could see we might be here awhile. Still kneeling at the projector, the other student was clearly trying to stifle something that was either a snicker or actual tears.

"The image looks completely fine to me," I said, replying as slowly as Lark had spoken. "What do you think is the problem with it?"

"It's completely unsaturated. Nothing looks the way it's supposed to." Lark had been standing with his arms crossed throughout this exchange, only now shifting so he could point at the screen and then the projector. "How is anyone supposed to be able to see my work in full when this thing isn't properly calibrated?"

I kept a smile plastered on my face as best I could, but I knew from much experience that my limit would soon be approaching.

"Could you please bring up the settings menu?" I asked the student. At the push of a few buttons, we could all see the settings as they were currently, including that the brightness and color saturation were both set to their max. I (politely) pointed this out to Lark.

"Well, it still looks like shit. Get a different projector," he said, going back to his arms-crossed stance.

My smile was gone. "This is the projector we use in all our classrooms. There isn't another model I can get." I was dimly aware that the room was starting to fill up as students and staff trickled in for the afternoon talk, but unfortunately this new audience wasn't enough for me to keep my cool any better.

Lark made an exasperated noise, like a sigh that he choked on. He could have cut quite the comical figure if he weren't so infuriating.

"The color is turned up to one hundred percent," I said. "There isn't any other projector in the building that will look any brighter than this."

Lark continued to stand there and stare me down. This was quite obviously not the first time he had had an exchange like this, and he had mastered the power of the silent treatment. Unfortunately, as he probably wanted, I took his lack of an answer as a direct affront.

"This is how projectors work," I could somehow hear myself yelling before I fully realized how loud my voice had gotten. "This is the projector we have. It's completely fine, and everyone else thinks so."

Lark's stare turned into an outright smirk. Apparently at some point the goal had moved from getting a new projector to seeing if he could make me lose my temper.

As I started to yell, Agnes had appeared at the podium, neatly swooping in and stepping between me and Lark. "Lark, it looks completely fine," she said. "We'll turn the lights down a bit once you get started and the colors will be fine." She murmured a few more conciliatory remarks, was met by a shrug that apparently meant he was backing down, then put her arm around me and walked us over to two empty seats.

Agnes leaned over to me once we were settled in our chairs. "Don't worry about him, Samantha," she whispered. "Lark is most comfortable when he can make everyone around him uncomfortable." She patted my hand and I managed a small smile, still feeling that peculiar combination of simmering anger mixed with embarrassment. Luckily, I was saved from further embarrassment as the lights dimmed and a hush came over the room.

The rest of his artist talk passed by uneventfully enough, with a pretty standard lecture about his major works, themes, and motivations. I tried to shake off any personal feelings and focus on the work on the screen, which currently showed a towering sheet of wavy plexiglass, held up by a minimal steel structure. The sculpture was set in an outdoor sculpture park, placed in such a way as to distort the view of a small lake just behind it, turning the water and surrounding trees into a wavy, psychedelic swirl of greens and blues as they filtered through the not-quite-clear plexiglas. As Lark pontificated on the history of land art, or sculptures set within and made of the landscape itself, I glanced around the room to see how my fellow students were taking it and whether they seemed to agree with his current proclamations as to his own place in this history. A quick look over my shoulder at Rebecca, my roommate, best friend, and mother hen, showed her toying with a pen in one hand, her other hand twirling her strawberry blond hair: a sure sign that Rebecca was deep in thought. Whether she was deep in thought about Lark or not, I couldn't guess. The rest of the auditorium showed students and a few professors in similar states of rapture (or drowsiness – it was hard to tell in the dim lighting).

I jolted back to attention as the lights brightened and a polite wave of applause swept through the room. Lark came out from behind the podium, genuflecting like an actual queen. I clapped along with everyone else, aware that my position in the second row meant that he had a clear view of Agnes and me. Luckily, I was able to turn my back soon as the rows behind us started to empty, and I could follow everyone else out to the reception.

I don't know why, but it really does seem like artists and the people around them – like the gallery assistant here whose job it was to set up the reception – love grapes and cheese more than anyone else. The modest cafe in our department building had been set up with a couple small tables with all the usual exhibit opening or art event fare: a few bottles of wine alongside a trio of plates with cheese, crackers and some fresh fruit. It was after five pm, so I felt justified in making a beeline for the wine, where Rebecca quickly fell in line beside me. I handed her a small plastic glass of white and asked what she thought of Lark's talk.

She shrugged. "Fine, I guess." She looked around the room, eyeing up the crowd. "It seems like a lot of people came, but I'm not sure what the big deal is, to be honest. His work is nice, but nothing extraordinary." Rebecca paused, considering, before giving another shrug. "Maybe it's just the kind of work you have to see in person. It doesn't translate well in photos."

Rebecca was always the more considerate, thoughtful one of us, which is really to say, I was sometimes too brash for my own good.

"Exactly. I don't know why he's here," I said. "Of all the people we could have had come this semester, why him? I thought his kind of work went out of style years ago. And if you were intent on highlighting work like that, there are so many other better examples of it."

She shot me an appraising look. "Mad about the projector still?" Rebecca grinned. "All good, Sam. He's a jerk – no one would blame you for erupting like that. Even I would probably have lost my cool."

I shifted on my feet uncomfortably, buying some time by popping a couple grapes in my mouth. "Whatever," I said at last. "I know that wasn't my finest moment." I nudged Rebecca with my elbow, nodding toward where Lark stood with Martina and a few students. Martina was beaming, apparently happy that he was fulfilling his visiting artist duties of mostly inspiring – and only occasionally whipping – students up into a frustrated rage. We stood watching while the students burst into laughter, Martina giving an indulgent smile. Even Rebecca rolled her eyes at that.

She drained the rest of her cup, tossing it into the nearest garbage can. "Should we get out of here? I could use an early dinner."

Rebecca looked at me expectantly, but I was distracted by the sight of Agnes and Lark together. She looked like she was on her way out, her coat already pulled on (a light wool number in black, naturally), and was saying her goodbyes. Goodbyes that included a somewhat unexpected pat on the arm and peck on the cheek.

"I'm actually heading over to Arun's tonight, but I'll catch up with you later at home," I said, quickly throwing on my coat (a ten-year-old worn canvas chore coat that was about one season away from threadbare, naturally) so I could try to walk out with Agnes.

Rebecca grinned, giving me a look that I knew from experience covered a much stronger urge to deliver a series of middle school taunts about my love life. "Why don't you bring Arun over?" she asked.

I gave her an equally knowing look.

"Your expression right now is exactly why I don't have him over more," I said, since we both knew that between her and Mel, our other roommate, any evening with Arun would be filled with the two of them circling around us, a pair of giggling, teasing lions, and Arun the poor antelope. I loved the two of them (or I loved Rebecca, dearly, and usually liked Mel, who could even herself admit to being occasionally grating), but there was something about seeing me with Arun that brought out a side of them I had mercifully been unfamiliar with so far. Sure, he was the older brother of one of my best friends. And yes, we had only been dating for about seven months, which, yes, did more or less coincide with him saving me from almost being killed in that aforementioned vat of chemicals. So, okay, I guess if you wanted to be all teenage girl about it, you could see Arun as my very handsome knight in shining armor mixed with a tiny dash of forbidden fruit (even though we had had Stephanie's, his sister's, complete approval). On the other hand, he was also simply the person I had had a huge crush on for nearly three years, and the last thing I wanted now was for my intrusive roommates to mess up everything.

Rebecca shrugged, already heading out of the building. "Whatever, Sam. You can't keep him away from us forever," she grinned, either in warning or promise.

I stepped outside with her, waving Rebecca to go on ahead of me as I walked over to where Agnes was still standing on the sidewalk. As the student she was chatting to walked off, I went over to join her.

"Thank you again for earlier," I said sheepishly. "I know I shouldn't always respond like that."

Agnes smiled kindly. "Not a problem, Samantha. Between us, I am firmly on your side. Lark has always been a bit difficult to handle. For some people."

A bit? Agnes wasn't usually prone to such understatement.

"I didn't know you knew him already," I said.

"Oh, I taught with him in Chicago before moving here. Many, many years ago, of course," she said.

Was it just me, or was she the one who now looked sheepish?

"I didn't know that. I can't imagine having to work with him every day," I replied.

"You got used to it," Agnes said and shrugged. "Lark just needs to feel attended to. But with enough people around who know how to manage him, he calms down." She paused, looking thoughtful. "There's another side to him, of course. Like anyone." Agnes shook her head, giving me a small smile as she seemed to break out of her reverie. "Well, Samantha, I had better be going. I'll see you around tomorrow?"

I nodded, waving, as she started off toward her car, and I turned, texting Arun that I was on my way.

Chapter 2

The next morning, I entered the sculpture studio as I usually do, first thing on Tuesday mornings. I turn on the lights, blink a few times in the overly bright fluorescents, and try to put my things down without spilling my coffee. Graceful as ever, that's me. But today, as the lights flickered on, I was greeted with a scene like something out of a '90s slasher film, and not one of the ones that's a funny spoof. The entire room was practically covered in blood, and something wasn't right. What's the right way for a room to be covered in blood, you ask? Fair question.

As my stomach climbed back up to its normal position after having dropped all the way to my feet, I regained at least a minimal sense of composure. So, although just moments before I was stumbling into the classroom like any other Tuesday morning, juggling a stack of handouts for the class, a large coffee, and miscellaneous supplies (because in art school you never know when you might need some plaster bandages or enamel paint), now I was standing in a room with a dead body. A man was lying prone near the front of the room, almost directly opposite the door, and judging from the amount of blood in the room, there was no way he was alive. So here was a dead body that no one else knew about yet. Well, that wasn't quite true, since whoever killed him probably knew. But no one knew about my being here. And you can call me crazy, but this seemed like a distinct advantage to me. (Okay, I'm definitely crazy.) But I had stumbled onto a murder scene that no one knew about yet, which meant that until I called for help, I was free to examine it. Every last bit.

Which might take some time, as the whole room seemed to be covered in evidence of what happened here. The chairs, ordinarily set up in pairs at a series of long tables, like the kind of table you might have had in your high school chemistry classroom, were now mostly overturned, strewn about the room as if a tornado had blown through. The tables themselves were pushed around at odd angles and no longer in a neat rectangle around the room. I inched forward, pulling out my phone to take a few pictures while being careful not to knock into any of the furniture.

It may seem like a fair question to ask at this point: What the hell did I think I was doing? Any normal person would probably have run screaming the second they turned on the lights and saw what had happened. But this wasn't the first time I had been confronted with a murder, and if that experience had taught me anything, it was that a thorough examination of the scene would yield information that, if I hadn't been so slow to come to my senses last time, could clearly point to the most likely culprit. Plus, it's not like I wasn't going to call the police. I definitely was. But that didn't mean I entirely trusted them to come to the right conclusion. Like last time, that murder they thought was a suicide only ended when the actual murderer tried to drown me in a vat of chemicals.

Having taken a few wide-angle shots to show the whole scene,

I crouched down in front of a large spattering of blood. The drops ran in even lines, forming concentric arcs like a rainbow. And this is what seemed instantly wrong to me about the whole scene. Not only was the blood laid out in neat patterns like this, as if the murder victim had willingly walked around the entire room, obligingly leaving their blood as directed, but the color didn't seem quite right. Dried blood is a relatively ugly color, an umber with a few drops of vermillion. This blood, on the other hand, was bright, a saturated red that stood out against the dinged, beige linoleum floor. Did people even have this much blood in them? Half the floor in the room was covered in patterns like this, plus most of the tabletops and chairs. It seemed too hard to believe that however this person had died, it had really happened in such a way as to create this precise scene.

As I stood back up, a bright flash of turquoise caught my eye. Gingerly stepping over the blood (even if it was fake somehow, I didn't want to be blamed for disturbing the scene), I took a few steps closer to what turned out to be a small pile of blue fibers, like a bored student had partially unraveled their scarf during class. Okay, I wasn't sure what that had to do with anything, but I took a picture nonetheless.

Aware that the clock was ticking and students might start to trickle in at any moment, I began making my way toward the front of the room. Even if I was increasingly sure the "blood" had to be paint, I did my best not to smear any of it as I crossed the room. The man was lying near the front wall, toward the right side of the room, where a teacher would stand while lecturing or directing a critique. This was probably meant to signify his importance or power, or maybe to arrange him like a body you'd be made to critique as if he were some junior's crappy homework assignment.

As I came closer to him, I realized with another shock who he was: Lark Harrier. My stomach started to sink again and I groaned inwardly as I realized that the last time I had seen him alive, I had been screaming at him in front of a room full of people.

Chapter 3

With the third mini heart attack of my Tuesday morning, I realized that the clock had been quickly ticking this whole time. Students would start coming into class soon, and this was very much not the scene I wanted them to walk into. Which meant it was time to call the police.

I continued to stand at the closed door to the classroom after the call was placed and the operator had assured me that officers would be arriving shortly. The first few students were starting to show up, and I directed them to go wait in the lobby for us. I didn't have time to think of a good excuse, so simply didn't offer one. It was too early in the morning for anyone to put up much of a fight, anyway. I didn't always cut the most commanding figure, but I assumed I could at least play off their exhaustion.

I honestly didn't know what to expect once the police arrived. Our last interactions had taken place in the spring and I wasn't exactly sure what kind of terms we had left on. No one involved had been rude or anything, but I can't imagine the police were thrilled that I'd correctly solved a case they had gotten so completely wrong. But at the sound of feet rushing up the stairs, I turned to see a plainclothes police detective, flanked by two uniformed officers and quickly followed by EMS workers, striding down the hallway. I'd find out soon enough.

"Detective O'Connor," I said, taking a deep breath to calm my stomach, which continued its elevator ride throughout my body. "It's just in here." I gestured to the closed door, standing back so everyone could go through.

Detective O'Connor hung back, letting EMS and his officers get in first. "Samantha, right?" he said. "I can't say it's quite nice to see you again, in circumstances like this."

I gave a small smile. "Didn't exactly plan for this."

O'Connor nodded, still studying me. He was fairly young, maybe forty at most, but from this distance I could see the fine lines around his eyes. His voice had a certain hoarseness to it that I assumed was exhaustion.

"What happened, exactly?" he asked. "We'll take a formal statement from you later, but for now just take me through this morning."

"Honestly, there's not very much to report about this morning. I got in at about eight-thirty am, the same as always, to set up for class. I'm the teaching assistant," I explained. "No one else was here yet, which is normal. Most kids don't show up until nine on the dot or later. I went inside, turned on the lights, and saw what had happened." I paused, not sure what further details I could really add. They would see for themselves what had happened soon enough.

O'Connor checked something on his phone. "So you go in at eight-thirty this morning?" He looked at me to confirm, which I did. "And you called 911 at eight-fifty am? So what happened in between?"

I stood up straight, tucking my shoulders back and trying to look like someone who was definitely not lying and would never think of lying; in reality, I probably looked like someone who knew they were about to tell a bald-faced lie and was owning it. "It was obviously a huge shock to walk in and see … everything," I said. "I must have stood there in shock for a few minutes before realizing what had happened, and once I did, I called 911 immediately."

O'Connor didn't say anything, just let me squirm under his careful gaze for a minute. No one could deny that it was a huge shock to walk into something like this. I stood firm, sticking to my explanation. At the very least, it was not a lie to say that I hadn't touched anything or removed evidence.

Luckily for me, the classroom door opened at that moment and the detective had a clear view of the scene inside. His look softened. "Okay, Samantha. We'll leave it at that. I know this kind of thing is never easy," he said. "Is there anything else you can tell me? Did you happen to recognize the deceased?"

At least this was a question I could answer honestly. "Lark Harrier," I said, spelling the last name for him. "He was here as a visiting artist in the art department." I then explained the program to O'Connor.

The detective looked thoughtful. "So would you say that it was public or even school-wide knowledge that he was here? Or was this a pretty department-specific program?"

"I think it's pretty much public knowledge," I replied. "The visiting artists usually choose to do a small exhibit here, or sometimes a public talk, so I think the gallery does advertise to the public."

O'Connor made a note of this. "Is there anything else you can tell me about Mr. Harrier? What was he like?"

I told the detective about Lark's work and the school in Chicago where he taught. As I finished, we were both aware that I had left the second question unanswered. Unfortunately, Detective O'Connor seemed very skilled at the whole silent-waiting, let-them-answer-in-their-own-time thing.

With a sigh, I decided that there was really nothing to be gained by my beating around the bush. "Lark was not a very nice person," I said. "He had a reputation as being something of a prima donna, and he definitely seemed to have earned that reputation fairly. I didn't have a whole lot of interaction with him, but what I did have was not particularly pleasant."

O'Connor was looking at me with his eyebrows raised, in an expression I couldn't read: either he was impressed at my honesty, or surprised I would be so stupid as to speak so negatively about a person whose body I had found that very morning.

"When was the last time you spoke with Mr. Harrier?" he asked.

Continuing to operate under the assumption that I had nothing to lose by simply telling the truth (and also knowing that the department gossip would get back to O'Connor sooner rather than later), I laid out the whole shouting about projectors incident from the day before.

"Honestly, I know it sounds like I really blew up at him, but this is pretty much how everyone's interactions have been with him the whole time Lark's been here," I reasoned. "After the artist talk, there was a small reception at the cafe downstairs. I left around six o'clock. That would've been the last time I saw him." I was spared from further questioning by the sight of Martina jogging down the hall toward us.

"Samantha!" she cried. "What on earth is going on? Are you all right?"

The classroom door opened at that moment as one of the

uniformed officers stepped out, and Martina tried to get a clear look inside. Detective O'Connor neatly swooped around her, stepping in to block the doorway.

"Ma'am, I'm afraid I'm going to have to ask you to step aside," he said, gently taking Martina by the arm and redirecting her to a spot farther down the hall. "Samantha here is completely fine, but there's been an incident and I can't have you going into the classroom at the moment."

Martina looked shocked, one hand clutching her chest and her face paler than I'd ever seen it. "What kind of incident?" she asked. "Is it a student?"

O'Connor sighed, looking at me. Correctly assuming that I wouldn't be able to hold off on telling Martina forever, he told her only that someone had been killed, but that it wasn't a student.

"May I have your full name, please?" he asked her. "And your business here this morning?"

"Martina St. Aubin. I teach the sculpture class that meets here. Sam is my assistant," she said. "But really, this is my classroom. My school. You need to tell me what really happened here." Martina could look quite fierce when she wanted to, and right now, I wouldn't have been able to look into that firmly resolved face and not given in.

O'Connor likewise relented. "I'm afraid it appears that Lark Harrier has been killed," he said.

"Oh my god," Martina cried, the anger going out of her instantly. "How could that happen? What happened to him?" she asked, her eyes already welling with tears.

"I'm afraid I really can't say anything further at this point. I'll have more details for you once we complete our examination of the scene," O'Connor replied firmly. "Samantha, will you please take Ms. St. Aubin to her office, or somewhere quiet she can wait? I'll need to speak with both of you again this morning, but for now I really need to get inside." He gestured to the classroom.

I nodded my agreement, already taking Martina by the arm.

"I believe I have your details already," he said to me, "I'll call you in about an hour when we need to speak."

I nodded again, and slowly started to maneuver Martina over to the stairs so we could go up to the faculty offices. The whole way there, Martina was silent, just slowly shaking her head.

It seemed like no sooner had I gotten Martina settled into her office with a cup of tea than my phone started blowing up. Not only was Detective O'Connor on his way up soon, but the students from that morning's class wanted to know what was going on.

I told Martina, asking if she was okay waiting for O'Connor alone while I went down to deal with the students. "Really?" I asked, feeling guilty at the thought of abandoning her, but relenting when she nodded.

"I'll be okay, Sam, really," Martina said, reaching out for my hand. "You've been very sweet this morning, when I know what a shock it must have been for you, too. You go down and tell the class we're obviously not meeting today but that they can expect to hear from me, maybe by tomorrow."

I nodded and headed downstairs, to address the veritable piranhas waiting for me.

Chapter 4

Okay, sure. You may think that after stumbling over a dead body, talking to a group of fifteen kids between the ages of eighteen and twenty would be the easiest thing. You'd be wrong! I sincerely hope that when I was a freshman (which I know it sounds a bit silly to say, since that was only three years ago), I was never as obnoxious as these kids. I actually loved being in class with them, helping them complete assignments and leading them through critique sessions. But when faced with seemingly straightforward conversation, they had a knack for turning everything on its head. I might have tried for some Agnes-level cool, calm, and collectedness, but more often than not I wound up a particularly unflattering shade of beet red while I tried to steer the conversation back on track.

I walked down the staircase slowly, aware that by the time I got to the lobby, the department gossip chain would already be in full swing. We were a medium-sized department in a much larger college, with a campus spread out across our Boston neighborhood. Unfortunately, being all cooped up in one building together meant that it was pretty much like living in a small town. A very small town.

I paused at the bottom of the stairs, where I could see the

students gathered around a couple of tables near the front door, but they hadn't noticed me just yet. I took out my phone to stall for time, texting Arun to see how he was and letting him know my morning had been "interesting" so far. A one-minute delay, and already I could hear my name being called from across the lobby.

I plastered on a smile that I hoped said: firm, in charge, but understanding and kind. "Hey, guys," I said, reaching the table around which my fifteen students sat and stood, with various expressions from bored to curious to angry at having been made to wait. "I'm afraid I have some bad news." I knew O'Connor would never forgive me for spilling the beans instantly, so figured I would stick with his "incident" line. "There was an incident earlier this morning in our classroom. Martina is okay, and everyone else in class is fine, but we're not going to be able to use the studio or meet today. Martina will be in touch tomorrow with some details and probably assignments for next week." I stopped, hoping this was enough information to pacify them for now.

"What kind of incident?" Matt asked. He was a sophomore I hadn't gotten to know very well yet, just enough to recognize that he usually exuded the kind of easy elegance I would have killed to have myself. But today, he was definitely one of the students who had gotten frustrated while waiting.

"I'm afraid I really can't say anything more specific. Again, everyone in class is fine; Martina and I are fine. But you probably saw the police come in. So I'm sure you'll understand that it's up to them now, and I really can't tell you anything else before the police decide it's okay."

The students grumbled, exchanging looks. "Did you find him?" a girl at the next table asked. She was a freshman whose name I was still struggling to remember. In my head, I usually called her Purple Hair, for obvious reasons.

"Find who?" I asked, genuinely surprised at her question.

"People are saying it's Lark Harrier." This was from Sofia, another freshman and a sweet girl who could always be counted on to say something positive during critiques.

I did my best to stop looking like a goldfish, but even I was shocked that the gossip had moved that quickly. I shut my mouth, debating whether to hold firm in my no comment stance or admit that the cat was already out of the bag. I could feel my phone going off in my pocket, which either meant that O'Connor was getting impatient or Arun was asking for details. In either case, these students' rumor mill was not what I needed to deal with right now.

"For the last time, I can't say anything other than that there's been an incident and we're not having class this week. I'm sure you'll hear more soon when the police decide to make a formal announcement. In the meantime, if you have questions about class work," I added, emphasizing "class work", "you can always email me."

With that, I turned and headed back to the stairs, not stopping until I was safely hidden in the stairwell. Before anything else, what I desperately needed was some quiet time to think.

Unfortunately, quiet time to think was the last thing I was going to get right now. My phone had been blowing up because of both Arun and O'Connor, which meant that I would have to face a lengthy phone call as soon as I left my interview with the detective, who seemed to have taken some kind of seminar since the last time he'd interviewed me, on how to ask the same question in as many different ways as possible.

And how to create a power imbalance in interviews, since I was currently sitting in a rickety student chair, while he was perched nonchalantly on a desk in the empty classroom the police had commandeered for interviews.

"I'm really not sure what else I can tell you," I was saying to O'Connor, not for the first time. "I already told you everything that happened this morning. It was all of thirty minutes, after all. I don't think I have anything else to add."

O'Connor looked at me thoughtfully, then back through his notes. "Okay," he said finally. "So all that happened this morning is that you found Lark Harrier in the sculpture classroom, as we've been through, and yesterday you had an altercation with him. But what about before then? Lark had been here for a week, Ms. St. Aubin tells us. What else happened in the past week?"

I paused, biting my tongue to keep from telling him again that "altercation" was too strong a word to describe the artist talk incident. Shouting match, maybe, if that still applied if only one person was shouting.

"Lark attended a few different sculpture classes. Mostly ones that Martina teaches, and I think one of Agnes's as well – that's Professor Pinel. And I think he did a few individual critique sessions, for some of the senior students. I didn't go, since you can only apply to two of the visiting artists each term and I'd already picked different artists," I said. Without trashing a dead man's reputation, what else could I tell O'Connor? "I wasn't there for every class, but from what I've heard, Lark acted much the same as he did during the artist talk. He just got under everybody's skin. Had pretty much nothing nice to say about anyone's work."

"Was there anyone who got particularly upset? Anyone who

got especially angry at him?"

"Not that I heard about," I said. "I think Martina would have mentioned it if there was anyone in her classes who really had a hard time. She could tell you better than I can."

O'Connor nodded, like he hadn't already asked Martina these very same questions. "And what about Lark's work? His life outside of Boston. Did you know him before he got here?"

I shook my head. "Lark teaches … Lark taught at an art school in Chicago, so I hadn't met him before. I knew his work a bit – he makes these large outdoor sculptures." I gestured to show the scale of his sculptures, rocking my chair precariously. "I didn't really know anything else. I didn't even know his reputation, but apparently how he behaved this week is pretty much the norm."

O'Connor snapped his notebook shut. "Okay, Sam. I appreciate the help, really. If you think of anything else, or if you hear anything, give me a call, okay?"

He waited till I nodded my agreement, then got up and let me make my escape.

Chapter 5

Our art department building wasn't huge and it was tough to find a place with any privacy, without having to venture out onto the roof or walk half a mile away. But there was one spot that I didn't even tell Rebecca about, where you could reliably find some peace and quiet: the basement level of the far back staircase. Was it comfy and warm? No. Was it perpetually cold, dank, and did it smell like a mix of old paint and dust? Yes. It was also the least trafficked area in the building, and where I was currently having a frantically whispered phone conversation with Arun.

"Sam, what?" he exploded. "You found a body? Are you okay? Do you want me to come meet you?"

I had just taken Arun through my morning. "No, thank you, really, I'm okay," I did my best to reassure him. "The police are here." *The same detective as last time*, I almost said, but didn't want to remind him how frequently I seemed to be in these situations. I don't know for sure, but that can't be the most attractive trait in a girlfriend. "I'm shaken up, a bit, but it's just a shock. It's not like he was my best friend, or anyone close to me."

"Still, Sam, that's a huge shock to have. To walk into first thing in the morning, too. Are you sure you don't want me to come get you? I can leave work early – it wouldn't be a problem," Arun offered. He worked as a journalist for a paper downtown, a quick subway ride from our campus.

"You're very sweet, really. But I have to go to work this afternoon. I missed a shift at the library last week and I can't afford to miss another so soon," I said. "But can I see you after? Maybe we can get dinner later?"

"Of course, Sam, anything you want," Arun replied. Despite my dank surroundings, I couldn't wipe the ridiculous grin off my face. "Just take it easy this afternoon, okay? If you need to go home early or anything, just give yourself a break, please?"

I promised I would, signing off with plans to meet at my house after work. Hanging up, I stayed where I was for a minute, offering some silent gratitude for having this person in my life.

I sighed. Break over, it was time to head up to work.

The library was my absolute favorite place in the building. Or one of the top three spots, at least, because it was hard to compete with the earthy, comforting smells of the pottery studio, or the bright, light-filled painting rooms. But the library had the best atmosphere, by far. It wasn't huge, just a few large rooms filled with thousands of books on art, framed by high windows and a set of couches. On a random weekday afternoon like this, the library would be about half full, with kids spread out on laptops at various tables or lounging on the couches with their textbooks open.

I settled in at the circulation desk and quickly got to work, helping a student who was waiting for help finding a list of books for their class. Between that, checking books in and out at a steady clip, and re-shelving a day's worth of returns, half the afternoon shift was already gone by the time I had a chance to sit down and think for a minute. I did a quick search for "Lark Harrier" in our library catalog, bringing up a couple of pages of search results. We had a few books about group exhibitions he had been in, plus one career retrospective of his work and the catalog for a solo exhibit. It was only fair that I might be a bit curious about this man who had stormed through our building and certainly had everyone's attention at this point.

I pulled the monograph and exhibit catalog off the shelf, starting with the monograph, a career retrospective of Lark's work that had been published a few years ago. I did the math quickly. Lark would have been in his early fifties when it was put together, maybe a bit young for a book like this. It was an attractive, hardcover volume with a wraparound photo on the cover showing a signature Lark Harrier sculpture: a wavy sheet of textured plexiglass that seemed to stretch on into infinity, nestled into a mound of grass and through which could be seen the blurry outlines of more grassy hills and trees. If nothing else, you couldn't deny that the guy's work looked great in photos.

I flipped past the introduction and image plates for now, skipping to the back where there was a brief biography and timeline of Lark's life. The biography was a classic of the artist monograph genre, something somehow succinct and over-the-top laudatory at once. From it I learned that Lark was born and raised in Maryland in the 1960s, in a seemingly average, middle-class family. He went to an art school in Baltimore for his undergraduate degree, then on to the Chicago art school, where he later taught, for a graduate degree in art and architecture. So, at least that helped explain how he could work out the engineering of all those precarious structures.

I didn't glean much more from the timeline, which was mostly a list of his major exhibitions and awards. It was a veritable who's who of art world institutions, with all the usual suspects represented. And it hardly even narrowed the timeframe in which he and Agnes could have taught together, since the timeline showed Lark teaching at Chicago from 1995 to the present.

I sighed, flipping back to the beginning of the book. I wasn't sure exactly what I was looking for, but it seemed somehow necessary that I should get to know this man better. If for no other reason than because he was an old acquaintance (old friend?) of Agnes, someone I admire deeply.

I turned the pages more slowly now, going through the images of Lark's work. I tried to keep as open and charitable a mind as possible, but with the images arranged in chronological order, it was clear that the guy had been doing pretty much the same work for several decades. Plexiglass in front of landscapes, plexiglass embedded in the landscape, photographs of plexiglass in the landscape hanging in a gallery. The most he strayed was in installations that combined photographs of his outdoor sculptures with piles of various landscape materials and boulders inside the gallery. Some of the sculptures were admittedly beautiful, transforming average vistas into painterly washes of blues and greens. But having seen one or two, did I need to see a hundred more?

I was interrupted at that moment by the sound of someone clearing their throat. I looked up to see Ricky standing at the circulation desk, tapping a pile of books she had just placed on the counter. I plastered on a smile, trying not to blush as I got up to check out her books. After all, I had nothing to be embarrassed about. I was just reading about our visiting artist.

"Is that Lark Harrier's work?" Ricky asked. "So awful what happened, isn't it?" Her voice was filled with faux concern.

I had gotten to know Ricky well while she was roommates with friends of ours last year, and after an incident in which I had riffled through her things (albeit with very good reasons in the course of figuring out who killed my friend), she and I were not exactly on the best of terms. Granted, she was no longer ignoring me outright – but we weren't exactly braiding each other's hair at slumber parties. But Ricky was staying on at school for an extra fifth-year program to get her teaching degree, so we would have to tolerate each other for just a while longer.

"Yep, it's awful," I said, going for a balance of caring but curt. I scanned in her books methodically, trying to signal that we didn't need to have a long, drawn-out conversation about this.

"Is it true you're the one who found him?" Ricky's eyes widened while I tried hard not to roll mine.

"Yeah, the rumors are true. I found him this morning. But I'm sure I don't have to tell you, I really can't say anything else right now. You know how this works," I reminded her. "It's up to the police now; I'm not allowed to say any more."

Ricky nodded solemnly. "Of course, I understand completely." She gathered up her books. "Just hope you're able to stay out of trouble this time." With that, she turned on her heel and strode out to the door.

I didn't even have a chance to say that I had no idea what she was talking about. I had zero reason to get involved in the investigation into Lark's death.

That said, it couldn't hurt to look through one more exhibition catalog. The thin volume was a petite square, with a simple image on the front that showed a stack of glass bricks with a thick white border. The exhibit had been done about two years ago, and looked like a slightly new direction for Lark's work. The gallery had hung several of his standard photographs of the outdoor plexiglass sculptures, but throughout the space were also several piles of materials, for lack of a better work: stacks of those same glass bricks, the blue-green glass cubes you used to see as dividing walls, along with a large boulder that had painted with thick white stripes and a few smaller piles of grass sod and dirt. I guess he was moving from sculptures set directly into the landscape to trying to bring the landscape into the gallery. The introductory essay didn't illuminate the topic much more, instead relying on a lot of the same details as the biography in his retrospective book. As I flipped the book closed, the name of the gallery on the back cover caught my eye. Giulia Lucerno was the name of the gallery, with an address in downtown Boston. I knew the general area pretty well, since there was a small cluster of galleries and art spaces in the area.

I started to wonder whether it might be worth a trip down there, then caught myself. It was like I would have said to Ricky: I had no reason to get involved.

Since it was only early October, the sun hadn't fully set by the time I left the library a little after five. I had just walked out the front doors, waving goodbye to the security guard at the front desk, and was about to put my earbuds in and turn on a podcast for the walk home when I noticed what was happening at the street in front of our building. I paused, pretending to be occupied by my phone while I watched as Detective O'Connor spoke with Agnes beside a cop car that was parked at the curb, with another officer standing nearby. I was too far away to hear anything that was being said. After another minute or so, I watched while the uniformed officer opened the back door of the car and Agnes got in. O'Connor got into the front seat, and the trio drove away. I was sure she was just going with them to help with some more questions, maybe provide a few other details about Lark's life since she seemed to be the only person around who really knew him. At least, that's what I told myself as I slowly started the walk home, finally turning on that podcast. I didn't hear a word of it the whole way home.

Chapter 6

As I walked in the front door of our triple-decker apartment, I could already hear that everyone else had beat me home. From our second-floor apartment came the sounds of music, Arun's deeper voice punctuating the percussion sounds of someone cooking.

I came in and headed straight to our kitchen, dropping my bag on the floor and kissing Arun hello. He had brought over a few pizzas, spread out on our kitchen table, while Rebecca was at the counter making a salad. Mel popped her head out of the pantry, holding up an open bottle of wine to me in greeting. I nodded, grateful, and settled in next to Arun, while Rebecca and Mel bustled around, bringing me wine and serving me more pizza than I could possibly eat.

"Thank you guys, really," I said. "This is exactly what I needed after today."

"Of course, Sam," Arun said. "How was your afternoon? You must be exhausted."

I nodded, trying to speak around a mouth full of molten cheese. "It was okay, the library was pretty quiet. I did a couple of interviews with the police this morning, but I didn't hear anything else from them the rest of the day."

At that, I certainly had Mel's attention. "People are saying the scene was a total nightmare. And the police have zero suspects. Is that true?"

"Mel, we talked about this. Give Sam a break." Rebecca glared at her, swatting Mel on the arm.

"What? It's not like Sam was besties with Lark. Nobody liked him. I was only asking what happened," Mel said and pouted. "You know, to set the rumors straight."

Even Arun had to roll his eyes at that. "Sam, you don't have to tell us anything you don't want to." He paused. "But actually, that said, there's a strong possibility I'm going to be assigned to cover this case. Would that be okay with you? Because I can pass on it if I have to."

"It's sweet of you to ask, but that would be completely fine," I said.

Arun had done an extensive write-up for his paper on everything that had happened last spring, so it made sense that his editor would want him on yet another story at our school. Plus, if he was on the beat, I'd have inside access to everything going on in the investigation. Not, you know, that I would need it.

"It should be easy for you, too, since the detective is that guy O'Connor, from last year," I said instead. "He was the one who showed up this morning."

"And what did he ask you about?" Mel tried again.

I held up my hand before Rebecca could hit her again. "It's fine, guys, really. It was a shock, but I'm okay. It wasn't as personal …" I trailed off, letting everyone fill in the blank. I gave them a rundown of my interviews from the morning, filling them in on the basics about Lark that I had gleaned from my afternoon at the library, while we slowly made headway on a second pizza.

"So it sounds like no one in the department had much of an obvious reason to kill Lark," Arun said. "Since basically no one knew him before he showed up this semester."

Mel shook her head vigorously. "That's not quite true," she said, leaning over the table towards us. "Do you know Charles? Year below us, a bit stocky, kind of looks like a younger Paul Rudd?" She continued once Rebecca and I nodded. "He and Lark had a huge blow up in one of Martina's classes last week. Charles stormed out of class, muttering all kinds of obscenities at him while Lark just stood there smirking."

"Where did you hear this?" Rebecca asked.

"Didn't hear it," Mel said, almost smugly. "I was there. I'm taking Martina's class on interactive sculpture, remember? Charles was showing this work he had been doing, or really doing in one of his performance art classes, but he usually brings it to Martina's for crit. And Lark went off at him, just absolutely trashed his work. Said all this stuff about how sculpture was for sculptors, not for silly actors who destroyed their own work to make a point about what, exactly?" Mel shrugged. "To be honest, I agreed with him. Charles can be so pompous, always calling everyone else's work 'kinetic objects,' while his are 'sculptural performance art pieces.'"

Arun frowned, considering. "How mad could this kid have possibly gotten? So one random visiting artist didn't think his work was any good. Would anyone really kill someone over that?"

The three of us all chimed in at the same time, speaking over one another to confirm that yes, absolutely, this was a distinct possibility.

"Critiques can get really heated," Rebecca explained. "A few weeks ago, I saw a kid in one of my painting classes get so upset while we were talking about his work that he threw a container of black paint at his canvas. It went everywhere, all over the painting, and he just stormed out."

I nodded. "In Martina's class during critiques, half the time I'm trying to get the students to say anything at all, and the other half I'm trying to keep them from rioting."

"I didn't realize class was basically a rugby match for you guys," Arun said, laughing.

"Intellectually at least, yeah," Rebecca confirmed. "Good analogy."

Mel and I agreed. "But listen, you guys, regardless of who got mad about what, and whatever Lark did or didn't do, it doesn't really matter, does it?" I said, to a table of confused faces. "What I'm trying to say is, the police will figure it out. What happened to Lark is a tragedy," I said, rushing on before Mel could cut in with something less charitable, "But it's just that. It doesn't have to be our tragedy, you know? It's up to the police now, anyway."

"Okay, Sam," Arun said. "Whatever you're comfortable with. We can leave it at that, right, ladies?" He looked to Mel and Rebecca for confirmation, which they gave (even if Mel needed a slight nudge).

We all promptly dropped the topic at the sight of Paul, the Phans' calico cat, slinking into the kitchen. The table turned into a chorus of oohs and aahs as Paul leapt onto an empty chair, turning on all the charm in the hopes of sharing in the cheesy goodness we were all incorrectly withholding from him. I grinned at the expression on Arun's face. Nothing brought out the adorable, nearly childlike side of him like a small animal.

I sighed, content. I was more than happy to leave the events of the day behind.

Chapter 7

I woke up the next day with the warmth of last night still happily lingering. So when I headed into school, I knew I would face a sea of rumors and gossip, but didn't expect anything much worse to come my way. I was happy to let the tide of pedestrian commuters sweep me all the way to our building, where I paused outside to share a cigarette with Mel before heading into class. Wednesday mornings had quickly become a favorite that semester, since I spent them in a small seminar Agnes was teaching on alternative materials.

But as I rounded the corner and stepped into the first studio door in the hall, I knew immediately something was off. Everyone else had beat me to class (not unusual), but Agnes wasn't in her customary place at the front of the room, where she usually sat amid a pile of example materials, a petite figure in between mounds of anything from styrofoam to paperclips. Today, Georgia, our grad student TA, was perched against the table in the front of the room, nervously fidgeting with her oversize glasses. I slid into a seat across from her, trying (and failing) to gracefully put my things down.

"Where's Agnes?" I asked Georgia, aware suddenly of the hush that had come over everyone else. I glanced behind me. The other ten students in class were sitting in twos at the rest of the work tables, each pair either exchanging glances or refusing to look up.

"Agnes can't make it in today," Georgia said, loudly enough to be an announcement for the whole class. "She had a prior commitment, so I'll be leading things today. I have some notes from her about your assignments. We'll start with our critique and then go over next week's work." She clapped her hands and signaled to us to gather around for critique, asking who wanted to go first.

I slipped quietly to the back as everyone gathered around a student seated at one of the front tables. It was obvious Georgia had been speaking with the shaky confidence of someone who knew they were lying. I, for one, did not believe that Agnes had some sudden, previously unannounced "prior commitment." My mind flashed back to the scene of her with Detective O'Connor outside school the night before.

With that image fresh in my mind, I grabbed my things and fled out the door before Georgia could say anything. I paused in the hallway to collect my thoughts: Who would know what was really going on?

At the top of the stairs to the third floor, I peeked around the corner and down the hallway that led to Martina's classroom. I had walked down this corridor countless times, but after yesterday morning, it had taken on an ominous undertone, seemingly darker than the rest of the building despite having the same skylights as the rest of the third floor. From the doorway to the stairwell, I could see two uniformed cops on duty, guarding the door to the classroom where I had found Lark. I took a moment to gather myself and tried to decide how best to approach the officers without simply storming out of the stairwell and demanding to see my teacher.

I plastered a warm smile on my face as I strode confidently down the hall toward the two men, or at least tried to look like that was what I was doing.

"Good morning, officers!" I said. "I was hoping to speak with Detective O'Connor. Is he in?" I tried to peer through the small window of the door to the classroom, but the officer on the right shifted to block my view.

"Detective O'Connor isn't on campus right now," the officer said. He was taller than his partner and looked just old enough to be the one in charge, or at least act like he was. "But we'll give you his card and you can always call to speak directly to him."

"Oh, of course. He must be really busy with Professor Pinel," I said, trying to take my most educated shot in the dark.

The younger officer nodded and opened his mouth to say something but was cut off by a glare from Officer Tall and in Charge. "Professor Pinel is assisting with our inquiries," he said. The younger officer nodded in confirmation.

"You can't really think Agnes has anything to do with this, can you?" I asked, addressing the younger officer directly. He couldn't have been more than a few years older than me, his features still holding onto a hint of baby fat.

He nodded before the other officer could cut him off.

"Detective O'Connor thinks the professor is our best lead right now," he said. His partner shot him a dark look.

"Oh come on," I said, trying for the easy-breezy tone of someone they could confide in. "Really? Does anyone really think that this tiny older lady could have anything to do with this? She couldn't make a scene like this, let alone take down a man that much bigger than her."

The older officer narrowed his eyes at me. "And how do you know what kind of scene it was?"

At least I had the grace to blush. "Well, I was actually the one to find Lark," I stammered. "So of course, I have somewhat of a vested interest in hearing what's going on now. I'm just concerned for Agnes, really. I couldn't see her doing something like this."

The officer didn't say anything, just fixed me with a stony look, although his younger partner squirmed as if he were trying hard to keep from speaking.

"But he was poisoned," the officer blurted out, receiving an ever-darkening look from his partner. "Anyone could have done it, an old lady even, anyone." He glanced to his left, taking in his partner's expression, and promptly turned a deep shade of lobster.

"Oh, don't worry about it," I said. "I won't tell anyone anything." *It's not like my boyfriend is a journalist or anything.*

"If you want to speak with Detective O'Connor, you can reach him at this number," the older officer said again, handing me a business card. "But now I'll need to ask you to step away from this classroom. It's an ongoing investigation."

"Absolutely, of course. Thank you, officers," I said, giving the younger one a small wave as I walked away.

I tried to walk calmly and not storm off with the full force of how angry I felt. But really, Agnes killing Lark? Agnes killing anyone? Hell, no. The idea was absurd. I admired Agnes more than pretty much anyone else and I knew without a sliver of a doubt that there was no way she would ever do anything like this. Or that she could even if she wanted to. I mean, did the police even look at the crime scene? Agnes was maybe two inches taller than me at most, which would put her at five five, maybe five six on a tall day. On top of which, she was in her early sixties, and I don't care how in shape she was. There was no way a petite older woman had torn through a room like that, flipping tables over and taking down a man who had to have at least forty pounds on her, poison or no poison. I could certainly maintain all my beliefs in girl power, while at the same time seeing that that situation seemed to defy the very laws of physics, let alone common sense.

I bounded back down the stairs towards the lobby. I needed to get some fresh air (and by get fresh air, I mean do the kind of thinking you can only do over a cigarette or several). I turned the corner into the lobby and saw Rebecca coming in through the front doors. At the sight of her worried expression, I knew instantly that the news about Agnes being suspect number one had made it all over the school already.

I motioned her over to me, ducking back around the corner so we wouldn't be in full view of the students who continued to trickle in late to morning classes.

"Sam, are you okay? I just heard that Agnes might be a suspect in … all this," Rebecca said, waving her arm vaguely.

I shook my head. "It's a joke," I said, taking her through all the reasons Agnes couldn't have done it. As I spoke, I could feel my resolve hardening. It was no joke, actually: It was a matter of defending someone who had never done anything even remotely close to this before and probably never even thought about doing something like this. I felt one tiny flutter of doubt at that. I mean, as far as I knew, Agnes had never thought about doing something like this.

Rebecca had been rubbing my arm with a sympathetic look while we were talking, but in that moment both her grip and her gaze hardened.

"No, Sam," she hissed. "I know that look." She tugged on my arm, as if to show how urgently I needed to stay where I was, not go running off. "You think you can bulldoze your way through all the ordinary procedures here, and go off on some kind of rescue mission. But that's not the way these things work." Rebecca's eyes pleaded with me to be sensible. "If Agnes didn't do it, she shouldn't have anything to worry about." I could understand and appreciate the concern, sincerely. But I erupted at this last sentiment.

"You and I both know that that's not always true." I could see in her face everything that lay unspoken between us: everything that had happened last semester, the friend we had lost and the aftermath of all that, still palpable in the undertones of everyone's gossip and stares, in the pseudo concern that was lobbed at us only as a ploy to get the "insider" details. Rebecca's look softened.

"I should know by now that I can never tell you what to do. But please, just promise me you'll be careful?"

"Of course, R. Really, it's not like I love rushing off into dangerous situations. But I do love Agnes, and this isn't right."

Rebecca bit her lip and nodded. "Whatever you do, just take Arun with you, okay?" She pulled me into a hug before I could get out a response.

It would have been half-hearted anyway –it might have been easy to say I didn't need a man to get basic tasks done, but it would have been hard to say I didn't need Arun.

Chapter 8

I t was a blessing to have to go to work that afternoon. The library was mercifully quiet, as the beautiful fall day we were having had drawn everyone outside with its warm autumn sunlight. Which meant that I was required to be in a peaceful space, with tasks to do, and some enforced quiet time, all of which ensured that I wouldn't go running off like a bull in a china shop. Rebecca was right that bulldozing my way through everything was not going to work in this situation. I needed to be methodical and move thoughtfully through this investigation, and I needed to sit, catch my breath, and calm down before I would be ready to do that.

It just infuriated me no end to think about what Agnes was going through right then. For all I knew, she had already been arrested or was at the very least being held at the police station, subjected to hours and hours of questions and interviews. She was kind and thoughtful enough to have volunteered her help, but did Agnes know what she was really getting into? I trusted Detective O'Connor, but I also knew what it was like when everyone around you wanted easy answers and shared a belief about how something had happened. I didn't want to think about what he could be pressured into doing.

I slid my phone out of my pocket, elbows resting on the

circulation desk as I tried to condense these thoughts into a coherent text to send to Arun. What was the right message for this moment? *Hi, honey, just wanted to let you know that I'll be hunting down a murderer to clear the name of my role model. Just so you know!* I didn't think that would quite cut it.

As I was still dithering, my phone started to vibrate.

"Hello?" I whispered, answering Arun's call.

"Hey, Sammy. I just wanted to see how you were doing," Arun replied. "Was class okay this morning?"

Class was not okay this morning, no. I told him about Agnes's absence, letting my pauses stretch on, hoping that he would fill in the blanks without my having to spell out what I was thinking or about to do. I stopped halfway through telling him about my questioning of the two police officers stationed at the classroom door. If you used a flirty smile to get information out of someone in the course of an investigation, was it okay to tell your boyfriend this? Why wasn't there a manual for this kind of thing? I mentally added this to my list of relationship questions to ask Rebecca.

"This sounds incredibly frustrating," Arun was saying, "I know how much you admire Agnes. I only met her the one time, but nothing about her exactly screams 'cold-blooded murderer,'" he said. Arun had gone to a gallery opening with me a few weeks ago, where introducing him to Agnes felt like I was introducing him to my parents, a moment with that same odd mix of embarrassment and hope. When Arun said he could see what I admired about her, I felt an almost childish kind of pride.

"The problem is, the police said that Lark was poisoned," I said, trying to whisper even more quietly as I became aware that the few students in the library were starting to look up at the sound of our conversation. "So even though it seems obvious that Agnes couldn't have attacked a man so much larger than her, the police don't think that matters if all she had to do was poison him."

Arun sighed. "I guess that attitude makes sense," he said. "After all, you do want to keep an open mind. Why don't I call the press officer and see what, if any of this, they can confirm?"

Not for the first time, I sent up a silent thanks for the good luck to be dating a journalist, and readily agreed that this would be the best next step.

"I just want to talk to Agnes more than anything," I said, gnawing on a cuticle. I knew I shouldn't let my anxiety get the better of me but it was tough to shake the feeling that I was already too far behind, that Agnes had already been caught up in the jaws of justice, or whatever metaphor you want to use.

"Listen, Sam, for all we know, Agnes really was just filling in some background information for the police and has already been released," Arun said. "I know it's hard, but it's really not worth panicking until we know what's really going on. The police officers on campus may not have the most up-to-date information, you know."

I nodded, but in all honesty I was only half-listening at this point. The other half of me was trying to figure how I would get Agnes alone, and where I'd even find her. I had been to her personal studio a couple of times before on class visits but wasn't sure what the ethics were of showing up announced, even with the offer to help clear her name.

"I'll let you know as soon as I get more information from the police press office," Arun was saying. "I have to work late tonight to make a deadline, but let's meet up tomorrow. I can come by campus on your lunch break?"

"That sounds great," I said, letting the relief wash over me as I realized that, no matter what, at least I wasn't alone in this. It's not every boyfriend who would stay this chill when their girlfriend announces she's going to investigate a murder.

"Of course, Sam, what else would I do? If you need help, I'm here," he said, signing off only after I'd promised to call him or check in if anything came up in the meantime.

I dropped back down into my chair, folding my arms on the circulation desk. I was about to lay my head down on my arms when a new stack of postcards sitting on the desk caught my eye. We often posted flyers or small cards advertising exhibitions in the library. The front of this postcard showed a bright abstract painting, a rectangle with rays of color shooting out from the center that looked as if it had been made in a computer paint program from twenty years ago. I smiled at the memory of sitting in my mom's classroom after school, where she would be grading homework for the fifth grade class she taught while I doodled on the computer. I was always partial to the paintbrush that made it look as if you were using a can of spray paint, even if my six-year-old self had never used an actual can of spray paint.

I frowned as I flipped the card over, then checked the date on my phone. The card advertised an event known locally as Third Thursday, when a group of galleries in downtown Boston all opened their doors, offering wine and cheese to the gallery-hopping crowd and usually hosting some kind of live event or opening for a new show. It was already October 20, which meant Third Thursday was tomorrow. My mind flashed back to the exhibition catalog I had found yesterday on Lark's work. It was still sitting on the book cart waiting to be reshelved, and I snatched it up, flipping to the copyright page.

I googled the name of the gallery, Giulia Lucerno, and saw that it was smackdab in the middle of the group of galleries that hosted Third Thursday.

I sent Arun a picture of the postcard laying on top of the exhibition catalog, asking if he fancied a trip out tomorrow night to Lark's gallery, and received a thumbs-up in return. I sighed, feeling at least some of the tension start to leave my body. Agnes might be with the police still, but at least we had a plan. Or the start of a plan. Or at least I hoped we did.

After work that evening, I let my feet walk me on autopilot to Stephanie and Arun's apartment, where I was promptly greeted with a mug of hot jasmine tea and ensconced on the couch with Stephanie. I loved my own mom, of course, but would always be thankful to have this home away from home at the Phans' apartment, where even the sounds of Sita cleaning up in the kitchen were a comfort.

Stephanie flipped through the channels, settling on one of those reality shows that are basically just glorified drinking games. She knew me well enough not to ask about what was going on at school. From the look on her face when I walked in, it was clear that Arun had already told her the basic details anyway. Stephanie just tossed a blanket to me and settled back, happy to watch silly television with me in comforting silence. With the warmth of the tea in my hands and the blanket over me, I felt my eyelids suddenly grow heavy. I knew there was so much work ahead of me if I was going to clear Agnes's name. But for now, there was nothing further to do. It couldn't hurt to just close my eyes for a moment, and fall asleep to the dulcet tones of housewives fighting.

Chapter 9

I spent most of the next morning in a state of leg-bouncing, jaw-clenching anticipation. I normally loved Martina's class on painted sculpture, but today all I wanted was to skip right to my lunch with Arun. I was greedy for information and couldn't wait to hear what he had gotten from the police.

I felt guilty for feeling so excited, especially when Martina looked downright haggard. She had smiled grimly when she came into class, sweeping a long gray coat and heavy bag of materials along behind her.

"Good morning, all," she said, leaving her things against the wall and standing in position in the front of the room. The frames of her black-rimmed glasses were thick, but not quite large enough to cover the dark bags ringing her eyes. Martina looked as if she had been up all night. Knowing her, she would have been awake worrying about Agnes.

"We all know this is a difficult time," Martina continued. "But I think it's important that we do our best to continue working. Lark showed us such a tremendous sense of dedication to his work. I think if we can continue in that spirit and remain focused on our work, it would be the most wonderful way to honor him." She paused, waiting for any comments. We were a small class, about a dozen people, none of whom was willing to interrupt or contradict her. "Okay, good. In that spirit, I believe today is Taylor's presentation, correct?" Martina asked, calling to a boy in the back of the room, who nodded, holding up a USB drive to show he had brought in his presentation. Each week, one of us was supposed to present on a specific type of "pictorial object," bringing into class a slideshow of related, representational sculptures or everyday objects (like the kid who brought in a presentation on the history of stop signs, a literal but definitely accurate interpretation of the theme). I somehow made it through the rest of the class without erupting in a mix of anxiety and excitement, dashing off to meet Arun as quickly as I could.

Although we weren't there to talk about the happiest subject, any anxiety about that morning evaporated as I settled in across from Arun. We were seated at a small table tucked in the front corner of a tiny coffee shop a few blocks away from campus, with Arun's notepad, two cups of coffee and the remnants of a shared cinnamon roll spread out between us. It might have been close to campus, but the cafe was tucked away on a small, mostly residential side street and I was grateful for the peace and quiet here.

"So, I spoke with O'Brien yesterday. Pat O'Brien, the press officer? I think I've mentioned him before," Arun said as he flipped through a few pages of notes. "Basically, the main thing he could tell me is that there is just a huge confusion over the scene itself. Apparently, there was such a massive amount of evidence found that they don't think it could all have been there naturally."

"What kind of evidence?"

"Fibers, hair, dirt – everything they've ever mentioned on

CSI," Arun grinned. "In a busy school building, you might expect to find a fair amount of that kind of evidence at the scene. But apparently, there was just so much that the police think a lot of it would have been planted."

I took a sip of coffee as I considered this, staring into the milky darkness as I tried to cast my mind back to the classroom when I'd found Lark. Remembering all the little piles of fibers and random objects strewn about, I could understand why there'd be some confusion. It had certainly looked like a huge mess, not the way the classrooms were ordinarily meant to be left.

"I don't think the police have figured out what was planted and what was there naturally," Arun continued. "To be honest, I don't think they even have a system for figuring it out. It sounds like a huge task, in fairness. If you've found a ton of stuff that you usually find at crime scenes, how can you tell what's supposed to be there and what was planted there if it all seems normal?"

I nodded, considering this. It seemed clear that the scene of the crime was meant to feel like a set, or a stage – something the murderer had constructed all around or for Lark. Or, simply that someone had gone to great pains to bring in a lot of miscellaneous evidence to cover up whatever tiny piece of actually incriminating evidence they must have left.

"What about the paint?" I asked. "Or the blood, whatever it was supposed to be."

"Yeah, I asked about that," Arun said, nodding. "It was definitely paint, something latex based." He paused, looking up from his notes and out the window as he seemed to consider his next words. I was anxious to hear what else Arun had found out, but can't say I wasn't always happy to have a chance to admire the strong jawline I'd been unabashedly lusting after for years. I'm only human. "Basically, the police think the whole scene is weird and artsy." Arun held up his hands when he saw the look on my face. "Not my words," he added. "But you have to admit, someone put a lot of work into making the classroom look the way it did. A lot of creative work."

"Sure, a lot of weird, artsy work," I said in a joking tone, although I was dead serious and deep in thought. "So, the murder was actually quiet and bloodless, a pretty simple poisoning, but the room was set up to make it look like a very different, much messier and more violent crime had been committed?"

"That pretty much sums it up," Arun confirmed. "Someone went to extremes to create a very specific scene around the murder. It would have taken a lot of time to paint in all the blood and make all the fake evidence." Arun looked thoughtful. "Whoever did this was very committed to appearances. Or at least to the appearance of this particular act."

I nodded, considering. "So, overall, a very theatrical and artistic crime scene?"

Arun nodded, then started slowly shaking his head as he already realized what I was going to say. I couldn't help but smile.

"Great, good thing it didn't take place in a building full of theatrical, artistic people!" I said, my voice rising enough to draw a few stares from the other customers. It sounded like a joke, but it was frustrating what a perfectly artistic crime this seemed to be. In any other setting, it could have been easy to find the most creative, the most artistic person – whoever was crazy enough to stick out. But at school, any one of us could have had the dedication to do this and to create a whole scene like this. We were an entire department of people committed to appearances.

Arun groaned. "I know, none of this helps narrow things down at all. The opposite, even. The police seem to think it's a needle in a haystack situation with the crime scene evidence."

"So how did they settle on Agnes? If it's such a messy scene, don't they have to process everything first before they can leap to accusing people?" I frowned. Arun reached across the table for my hand, his grip firm and comforting.

"Sam, no one has been accused of anything," Arun said softly. "Agnes is fine. She spent a couple of days answering the police's questions about Lark, since she was the main person here who knew him before his visit." Arun paused, clearly mulling over how much more to tell me. I stayed silent, willing him to tell me everything but not quite able to bring myself to ask him to.

"But it's true the police have zeroed in on Agnes. They do see her as a strong suspect," Arun said. "I asked if they were detaining anyone or if they had identified a suspect, and O'Brien wouldn't confirm or deny, just fell back on his line about it being an ongoing investigation. But when I asked about Agnes specifically, it was pretty clear what he thought."

I still couldn't say anything, just sat there shaking my head. I could feel my jaw clenching hard enough that I should probably have had my dentist on speed dial.

"Listen, Sam," Arun said, leaning closer over the table. "Agnes told the police that she and Lark used to be in a relationship. A pretty serious relationship, it sounds like. I think they broke up around the time she left Chicago. So the police are seeing it as a revenge motive, assuming that Agnes was distraught when they split, and she killed him now out of jealousy or to get back at him …" Arun shrugged. "I know it sounds like a weak motive, especially for Agnes. But the police don't know her well and she's the only person they've found who had any connection to Lark before he got here."

I sat there silently, the first words of sentences flying through my mind as I tried to figure out how to respond to that. Arun's expression made it clear he understood what was going through my mind. I shook my head.

"Why would Agnes wait a decade to kill him? If she was so upset when they broke up, why didn't she just kill him at that moment?" I asked. Arun shrugged, shaking his head.

"I know," he said. "It sounds like a ridiculous proposition. But that's all the police have. At least for right now. They're still interviewing people and checking into anyone who had anything to do with Lark on campus."

I felt guilty wishing that they would find anything that could take the spotlight off of Agnes. I wouldn't wish this feeling on anyone else, obviously no one who wasn't guilty, but I couldn't stand the idea of Agnes feeling trapped, cornered by the police just because she once knew someone who had the unfortunate luck to get murdered in the building where she worked. Which, sure, when you said it like that, did make the police's perspective seem a little bit more reasonable. Only a little.

"We'll figure it out," I said, my voice sounding more resolved than I really felt. "If we know for sure that Agnes didn't do it, then it won't be hard to find the person who really did. Process of elimination, right?" I grinned. "No matter how many crazy artists we have to wade through."

"Exactly," Arun said, returning my grin. "I'll be here to help as you suffer through every bad critique and boring exhibit, right?"

I squeezed his hand, genuinely grateful despite my joking

tone. "Great. Speaking of which, you still up for Third Thursday tonight?"

"Definitely," Arun said. "But I'm afraid I should get going now." He checked the time on his phone, then hurried to gather his things. "I didn't realize how late it had gotten. I have to get back for a one o'clock editorial meeting." He stood up, suddenly towering over me. "Meet you at six tonight?"

I nodded, tilting my head up so he could kiss me goodbye. I watched as he left the coffee shop, appreciating his confident, long strides and the wave he gave me through the window. I stayed where I was, pulling his unfinished coffee and the rest of our pastry over to me. I didn't have class that afternoon and although I knew I had a mountain of work to get through in the pottery studio (or, okay, a tiny mountain made of miniatures), I wasn't quite ready to go back to school. The coffee shop had emptied a bit after the lunch rush, with maybe a dozen customers in the sunny space. It was as calm and pleasant a place as any to continue thinking about a dead visiting artist.

I rummaged in my bag, digging under an extra sweater and scarf (it was drafty around our old art department building), then wedging my hand under a pile of library books to finally extract my sketchbook. I probably went through two or three sketchbooks each school year, filling at least one up each semester with notes, silly sketches, plans for assignments, less silly sketches. Now, as I cracked the spine of the red fabric bound book and smoothed out the blank pages, I knew what I had to draw: the scene of the crime.

For as long as I can remember, I've turned to drawing when I can't understand something or when I want to commit something to memory. I've used it for everything from those difficult word problems in fifth grade math class to remembering the chronological order of artists for an art history quiz (some other time I'll show you my sketches of male Renaissance artists all in drag, naturally, since it's easier to remember things once you've put your own spin on it).

In the top left corner of the page, I added two lines to indicate the doorway that I had walked through that Tuesday morning. On the opposite wall, there was a second door that led directly into the pottery studio. I treated the top of the page as the front wall of the classroom, and followed the wall from the door over to the opposite corner, where Lark had been lying. Whatever you could have said about the guy in life (and probably wanted to), it didn't feel right to skip over this part of the drawing. I hadn't examined him from too close up, but could remember the simplicity of his posture, the way his legs had been straight out in front of him, with one arm flung over his chest and the other continuing the gesture, pointing out away from him. Lark had worn minimal, wire-rimmed glasses which I assumed had been knocked off when he fell; they were lying a couple feet away from him, but were unbroken.

I scrolled through the photos on my phone, looking at the ones I had taken in the classroom. It was funny how different our memories could be from what really happened. I would have sworn that I had a nearly photographic memory of the classroom that morning, but looking at the actual photos now, it seemed like the scene was much simpler than my memory of it. I guess in the moment, my mental snapshot had had an extra layer of shock imbuing the image.

In reality, the way the tables and chairs were strewn about no longer seemed random, like a tornado had blown through the small space. Sketching the furniture in now with quick, dark lines (in a soft, rich 4B pencil, for those of you wondering; not necessarily my top choice, but the only thing I could dig out of the depths of my backpack), a clearer picture emerged. There were four tables in the room, with three on their sides and one completely upside down. Interspersed around them were about ten chairs, with another half-dozen chairs stacked in the back of the room, where they were normally kept. Looking down at the drawing, the furniture wasn't tossed around in a random pattern, as it had seemed at the moment: Instead, the tables seemed to almost point towards Lark, forming two parallel lines that moved diagonally across the room and towards the spot where Lark had been lying. The chairs were more scattered, but still followed this general arrangement.

This realization was very well and good, but what the hell did it mean? I looked up, letting the sunlight and pale autumn sky act as a palette cleanser. Outside, the street was quiet, just a few people walking around on their normal, everyday errands and work, probably none of which involved murder. Probably.

Maybe what was missing was color. I rooted around my bag for a small pencil case that held a set of colored pencils I'd had for nearly a decade. Most had been sharpened all the way down to nubs that were barely the size of those pencils you'd use on a golf course, but nothing was too miniature for me. In a few quick strokes, I added in bright, dashed lines of cadmium red to show more or less where the faux blood had been painted in. Unlike the tables, the pattern of the blood revealed nothing to me. Or at least there was certainly no order to it that was apparent, as it swooped and swirled all over the floor and most of the furniture.

I sighed, picking up and putting down the still uneaten cinnamon bun. Normally, I loved every kind of faux, fake, replica anything you could possibly imagine, especially if it had been sized down to miniature. But this was just too much. Someone had not only taken care to create this scene, but had spent a hell of a lot of time doing so. I shuddered at the thought of an hour spent painting fake blood in a classroom while Lark lay dead at the front.

The sunlight streaming in through the window was barely bright enough to wash away the creepiness. But at least one thing had become apparent: There was so much "evidence" created, that it seemed likely at least some of the materials were still on campus. Most of the students in the art department avoided the cramped dorms and lived off campus, opting to live together in whatever apartments we could afford, all over the city. So there was a reason we had lockers on campus, since no one wanted to lug a ton of heavy supplies back and forth across Boston every day. Which meant that if someone had created this much fake evidence, they had either managed to carry everything away with them without being noticed or, hopefully, they had left some evidence of their criminal crafting on campus. All I had to do was find it.

Chapter 10

For better or worse, there was one major event I had to get through before I would get a chance to search the sculpture studios for any "evidence" materials left behind. Third Thursday in Boston's art district was a monthly institution among certain crowds, offering the chance to see and be seen against a backdrop of new art installations, exhibit openings, and whatever art dealer wheelings and dealings went on behind the scenes. Unfortunately, all that see-and-be-seen-business meant that I had to spend some serious time getting ready, allowing (okay, begging) Rebecca to use whatever magic potions she hid in our bathroom cabinet to tame the curly bird's nest of my hair (and skin, and face …).

I'm not normally a particularly girly girl, if that isn't already obvious, but even I had to admit that the time spent getting ready together was (almost) worth it when I saw the appreciative grin on Arun's face when he met me and Rebecca, a couple of blocks from where the Third Thursday galleries were. I fought off the urge to twirl around and show off my outfit (a grey-and-black-striped tunic over slim black pants with one of Rebecca's colorful, bulbous necklaces), instead getting up on tiptoe to kiss him hello. We walked the few blocks over to the galleries mostly silently, avoiding any talk about Lark, aware that even if we were off campus, Boston was a small town and anyone could overhear at pretty much any point.

Giulia Lucerno's gallery was a jewel box of a space, tucked between two other galleries right in the middle of the arts district. The warm wood floors and dim lighting created an inviting, warm atmosphere, only somewhat tempered by the memorial-like vibes going on. I had suggested we stop in at another gallery first and not look like we were making a beeline for Lark's gallery, but clearly I hadn't needed to worry about how that would look. The small gallery was already packed, with people milling around, speaking in hushed tones, wine in hand.

The three of us walked in, Rebecca heading over to a fellow gallery intern she recognized while Arun and I did a quick circuit of the room. The gallery had hastily hung a small collection of Lark's photographs, most showing his outdoor sculptures at various angles and against different landscapes.

"Is this what all of his work was like?" Arun asked. From his studiously neutral tone, I couldn't quite tell whether it would be a good or bad thing if it was.

"More or less," I said. "The sculptures in these photos were his main work. Lark's whole career was spent on these huge, outdoor works."

Arun nodded, still not giving away his opinion. I guess you don't really want to be the one person at a memorial bad-mouthing the deceased. I pulled Arun over to the side, finding a good spot in the corner of the room where we would have the best vantage point to see who was coming in and out.

Arun surveyed the crowd for a minute, taking in the scene as people moved from photo to photo, small groups forming and breaking up as old friends ran into each other, then moved aside to let others through the small space. Pretty much everyone here was under thirty, with the occasional elegant older couple sprinkled in.

"Do you know which one Giulia is?" Arun asked, leaning down to ask me quietly.

I looked around, considering each of the older women in turn.

"My best guess is the woman at three o'clock," I said, nodding toward the far right wall, where a tall brunette was holding court over a group of five or six people. Her hair was piled up in a dramatic, messy bouffant, matched by the puffs of the sleeves on her long black dress. Everything about her screamed drama, especially the loud, vaguely European voice in which she was currently bemoaning something, presumably Lark's death, to the group.

Arun nodded, biting back a smile. "Definitely who I would pick to play a gallery owner if I was casting for a movie."

I elbowed him lightly.

"I did a quick search before we got here," I said. "It looks like she's been open for almost twenty years. Not always in this exact space, but always in Boston." I paused, considering how good this woman looked for what I now realized must be her age, and how impressively young she must have been when she got started. "She's been Lark's gallerist from the very start. He's never been represented by anyone else." Which meant, I thought, that Giulia must be one heck of a gallerist. Most other well-known artists seemed to pick up gallery representation around the world, as if that were a normal souvenir most people collected. I said as much to Arun.

"So what are we looking for here, exactly?" Arun asked.

"Why don't you walk around, ask some questions about

Lark?" I replied. "Or at least hear what people are saying. You know, really put those journalist skills to good use." I grinned as he rolled his eyes at me. "I'm going to see if I can snoop around in the back at all," I said, craning my neck to see down a short hallway on our right. "There's always some kind of back storage room or office at these galleries. Maybe I can find something useful."

"Okay, let's meet out front in fifteen minutes. Be careful," Arun said, giving my hand a squeeze as we drifted off, with him moving off towards a small group next to us while I casually headed over to the hallway that I hoped led to Giulia's office, or whatever inner sanctum where she'd hopefully hidden a bunch of Lark-related clues.

I stood in front of a photo showing a bright red square, cut out like a frame, that was positioned in front of a range of desert mountains, pretending to study the image as I slowly edged to the entrance of the hallway. I took a quick look around. Everyone seemed engrossed in either conversation or looking at the photographs and Giulia was still going strong with whatever story she was currently telling, one that seemed to rely on a lot of hand gestures. I took the opportunity to slip out of the room, hurrying down the hall and hopefully out of sight.

The hallway ended with two doorways on either side. I tried the door on the right: locked. Which was fine, since it was probably just their storage space. If I wanted private papers, I'd need an office.

Which luckily was exactly what door number two was. The door swung open creakily, stopped short by a stack of bankers boxes piled against the wall. I stepped inside, clicking the door shut behind me and allowing my eyes a minute to adjust to the dim, dusty light filtering through the small window.

Office was a generous term for the space I currently found myself in. Broom closet may have been a more accurate term, since I could reach my arms out and almost touch both walls at once. It was a pretty bare-bones room, with the only furniture being a small desk and desk chair against the back wall, with an extra chair tucked on the other side of the desk. Shelves lined one wall, stacked high with the detritus of twenty years in business: piles of paper, file folders, books and exhibition catalogs, plus an assortment of small sculptures and prints sitting propped against the wall. The desk itself was pretty much bare, with just a single laptop out.

I walked around the desk, hoping for some neatly organized drawers with files labeled something like "What I Really Think About Lark Harrier," or "How Lark Harrier Wronged Me." Obviously, I had no such luck. The drawers were as much of a mess as the shelves, stuffed with every piece of hardware and miscellaneous tool you might need to install an exhibit.

I had just picked up a small stack of papers from the shelf closest to me when I heard footsteps coming down the hallway. I had just enough time to shove the papers back in place when the door swung open. Or as open as the mess would allow. Spotlit in the doorway stood a slim girl about my age, with pin straight blond hair and dressed in a short black dress.

"Can I help you?" she asked, in a tone that made it very clear that I was not supposed to be here.

"Sorry!" I grinned brightly, hoping to come across as a slightly wine-drunk, definitely harmless idiot. "I was just looking for the bathroom," I said. Everyone's favorite excuse for being where they shouldn't be.

Her eyes narrowed. "There isn't a public restroom here, I'm

afraid. You'll have to go to the coffee shop across the street." She stood back, holding the door open for me in a clear signal that I needed to leave. Immediately.

I didn't hesitate. "Right, thanks so much!" I said, still as brightly as I could muster. I headed back out through the gallery, which was still as crowded as ever. I saw Arun out of the corner of my eye, where he looked to be feigning interest in something an older man was wildly gesticulating about. I gave a small shake of my head to indicate that I hadn't found anything, and stepped out into the now chilly October evening.

Not only had I not found anything definitive, I wasn't even sure what there was to find. Love letters to Lark and a scorned or soured romance? Blackmail? I sighed, wandering over to a bench on the sidewalk nearby. I knew gallery owner-artist relationships were complicated, but complicated enough to result in murder?

The only thing I knew for sure was that there was a huge contrast between the warm, inviting and bustling gallery space with its expensive lighting and even more expensively framed photos, and the tiny, cramped and messy closet that Giulia called an office. The discord made the scene in the gallery look like a show, a theater set Giulia had constructed to paper over the reality of a business with high costs and small margins.

"No luck?" Arun said as he plunked down next to me, handing me a small plastic glass of wine which I accepted gratefully.

"No luck," I confirmed, telling him about the gallery assistant who interrupted me. "Did you hear anything useful?"

"I think so," Arun said slowly. "But I'm honestly not sure what any of it means yet. A lot of people were talking about Lark, as to be expected." He paused as a trio of art department students came down the sidewalk towards us, waving hello to me. I said my hellos as quickly as I could, nudging Arun to get back to his story.

"A couple of people said things along the lines of, 'I'm impressed that Giulia managed to get this show up,' or 'I'm glad to see she's still here," Arun recited. "I asked one person what he meant by this and apparently, Giulia's been having money trouble. It must have been going on for some time since it sounds like this isn't the first time that there's been rumors going around about her closing." Arun grinned. "Then I got quite the lecture about the economics of the art market for small art dealers."

"It's not surprising that Giulia was having money problems. At least one or two galleries over here close every year. And there's usually another gallery that's ready to come up right after them, but most don't last as long as she has." I paused, considering. "But I don't see what Giulia's money problems would have to do with Lark. Especially with any reason to kill him."

"Maybe she was trying to get money from him?" Arun offered. "Or he was somehow pressuring her into staying open?"

"It would have been the other way around," said a voice behind us. I leapt up, spinning around as Arun held up an arm across me, moving to stand slightly in front of me.

James Thompson. Professor Thompson, that is, stood in front of us with his phone in one hand and a cigarette in the other, a pretty much permanent smirk on his face. Thompson had been a professor of my friend who was killed last semester, though I had successfully avoided working with him myself so far. The man was smarmy at best, a creepy pervert at worst. Which, come to think of it, probably made him perfect for analyzing Lark.

"What do you mean, the other way around?" I asked, trying to speak confidently and not like someone who'd just had a jump scare.

Thompson shrugged. "Lark wouldn't have pressured Giulia into staying open. He was probably going to leave her, sooner or later."

"Why? Isn't this how he made money?" Arun said, gesturing to the scene inside.

"Yes and no," Thompson replied. "He made money selling work, sure. But he could have made a lot more money with the right gallery." He glanced over his shoulder, surveying the gallery. "Giulia is a solid gallerist. She's been here a long time, definitely knows how everything works and has good instincts on what will sell and what won't. But Lark had been ready for the big leagues for a long time," Thompson paused to take a dramatically long drag of his cigarette. "Giulia had been his gallerist from day one. When he couldn't even get the time of day from any of the New York City galleries." Thompson shrugged. "But Lark was ready to move up."

"Isn't your gallery only in Boston?" I asked. Snarky, sure, but I didn't want to talk to this man any longer than I had to. Even if what he said had the distinct ring of truth to it.

Thompson's smirk turned into a grin. "Yes, Sam," he said, pointing down the street to a bright white storefront whose glaring fluorescents spilled out of a picture window framing a bustling crowd inside. "I'm with Primary Pictures. And some day, I'll probably move on too. Like Lark should have." With that, Thompson flicked his cigarette butt away and turned on his heel, giving us a small wave as he headed off to his gallery.

I sunk back down on the bench, gulping the rest of my wine down and taking out a cigarette of my own.

"Do you believe him?" Arun asked. "Do people usually change galleries like that?"

I hated to admit it, but Thompson was definitely onto something. I nodded begrudgingly. "I was honestly thinking about that when I was trying to get into Giulia's office. Artists who show as much and as internationally as Lark did usually have global representation. You know, their gallerist in London, their gallerist in New York, and so on. At least two or three."

"So if Lark was looking around for another gallery, how quickly would Giulia have found out?" Arun asked.

"Honestly, she probably knew immediately. Even if he never told her directly, it's a small, small world. If Lark was talking to other galleries, it would have gotten back to Giulia almost immediately."

"But why kill him?" Arun frowned. "If you didn't want him to leave your gallery, I don't see how killing him would have helped anything."

I shook my head, feeling conflicted over how excited I felt about this potential motive, even when it represented what was a pretty sorry state of affairs for artists. "Lark dying would have actually been the best thing for Giulia, in this situation," I explained. "If he moved to another gallery, she would have lost a lot of money. But if he died before leaving her, Giulia stood to make a small fortune." I finished the cigarette, pausing to neatly grind it out under my foot, then continuing when I saw how confused Arun still looked.

"Lark's work is about to get a whole lot more valuable now that he's dead," I said matter-of-factly. "Honestly, it may even be more valuable since he was murdered."

Arun shook his head. "Right. So if you were Giulia, or presumably any other small, struggling gallery, the best thing for you would be if one or more of your artists died?"

"Well it would probably look suspicious if too many of them died," I said, laughing. "But yeah, that pretty much sums it up. The most valuable kind of artist to be, or to represent as a gallery, is a dead artist."

We were interrupted from further reflection on this lovely, lighthearted topic at the sight of Rebecca coming over to us.

"Hey, sorry I lost you guys in there," she said, pulling her coat more tightly shut against the chilly October evening. "That was Tia, a girl who works down the street," Rebecca said, gesturing vaguely at another gallery on the block. "She said all the gallery owners, and everybody else around here, are talking about nothing except Lark."

"Did she mention if anyone was particularly upset or had any kind of weird reaction?" Arun asked. "Maybe not something as obvious as someone being openly overjoyed that Lark died, but, you know. Anything like that."

Rebecca shook her head. "No, Tia was pretty shocked about it herself. But I'm having coffee with her after work tomorrow, so I can ask her more about it then," Rebecca said. "Did you guys find anything interesting?"

I gave her the rundown, skipping the part where I technically broke into Giulia's office (although the door was unlocked, so it was only some light trespassing); I loved Rebecca, but she always worried about silly things like breaking and entering, so it was probably better that she not know.

"I think that makes a lot of sense," she said as I finished telling her what Thompson had thought about Lark leaving. "I can lightly ask around during work tomorrow. Betsy is the biggest gossip I've ever met, so if anyone would know about Giulia's money problems, it would be her." Betsy was Rebecca's boss at the gallery she worked at, named eponymously for her: Betsy Gilbert. She was a character if there ever was one, a woman whose clothes were usually loud enough to match her voice. I mean, the woman had a full rainbow of matching hats and purses that she rotated through on a daily basis. To be matched by her collection of oversized, colorful glasses, naturally.

Before Rebecca could recount the latest Betsy story, we were interrupted by a couple coming out of Giulia's gallery.

"Leah, hi!" I said, greeting the grad student who TA'd one of the art history courses I was taking that semester, on design and nature (that, yes, was called "Bees, Butterflies and Bauhaus"). I didn't know her especially well but she was always friendly, her perky demeanor somehow accented by a pixie cut and bright, rainbow colored glasses.

"Hi Sam, how're you guys doing?" Leah said, greeting Rebecca and Arun. "This is Cam," she gestured to the man she was with, who gave a sullen nod.

"Nice to meet you," I said, trying hard to picture my usually bright, happy TA with this sullen, bordering on rude, man. Although, he looked enough like Arun with his short black hair and sharp cheekbones that I did have to admit I could see the appeal.

"Did you guys know Lark?" I nodded towards the gallery. "What did you think of the show?"

Cam snorted as Leah shot him a quick look. "I thought the show was beautifully done," Leah said graciously. "Lark was actually Cam's business partner," she continued, hesitantly looking at Cam as if to ask permission for telling us.

"Oh, wow. I'm sorry for your loss then," Arun said. "What business were you guys launching? I had no idea that Lark was involved in anything like that."

"It's a collaborative workplace venture," Cam replied curtly. "Lark was supposed to be a shadow partner."

"What's that in normal English?" Arun whispered to me as I stifled a laugh.

"So are you going to be able to continue with the business? Now that Lark's…uh. Not here," I fumbled.

Cam gave another of what had to be his signature curt nods. "As I said, he was a shadow partner. He had barely contributed anything as it was. We're opening in a couple of months, just a few blocks away actually."

"Oh, that's great," Rebecca said. "Maybe we could come check out the space sometime. We're graduating this year so we'll probably need studio space pretty soon." I looked at her in surprise. Apparently Rebecca was more on board with this whole investigating people's murders thing than I thought.

"Of course, you can come by anytime. We're still kitting out each of the workspaces but you'll be able to see the general structure of the space," Cam said as he handed out business cards.

"Well this is great, I'm glad we ran into you guys! Hope to see you at Cam's new spot sometime soon!" Leah waved as she and Cam turned to go.

I waited until they were farther down the block before turning to Arun to answer his previous question. "It's a building with studio spaces to rent," I said. "And maybe some shared tools you can use."

"Ah, yeah. I'm curious what kind of capital something like that would take," Arun said. "He and Lark must have raised a lot of investor money to fund a building renovation, if that's what he meant about kitting out the space."

"But it sounds like Lark contributed hardly anything," Rebecca said. "To be honest, from everything I've heard about him, it definitely sounds like Lark was the kind of person to promise one thing and do another."

"Agreed," said Arun. "I'm curious enough about this business that I'll do some digging. If nothing else, I should be able to see from the forms they have to file with the state who actually owned the business. If Lark was a shadow partner and not a joint owner, he may not have been on all the paperwork," Arun said slowly, considering. "Which means, if there were any kind of financial issues, Cam would be the one left holding the bag."

I nodded. "And whatever the story is there, he was definitely more angry than sad about Lark. I think that definitely bears some further looking into." Rebecca agreed.

"I don't know exactly what I was expecting to find tonight, but I don't think it was a whole mess of financial motives for Lark's death," I said.

"Well, that's why they always say to follow the money," Arun replied. "But what if we took a break for now? We could follow the wine instead," he said, smiling. As if on cue, my stomach growled. Who was I to turn down some free wine and cheese? I threaded my arm through his and let Arun lead the way to hors d'oeuvres.

Chapter 11

As much as I might have enjoyed the wine and snacks of the night before, I wasn't exactly enjoying the fuzzy headed grogginess I had now. I had chugged a huge bottle of water on my run into class and was now standing in the studio clutching the largest coffee our department's small cafe had to offer, trying to inconspicuously take enormous gulps between replying to Martina – in what I hoped was the voice of an adult person not currently hungover. We were meeting for class in the woodshop today so the students could get the necessary training to be able to use all the tools, and the last thing anyone needed was a clumsy, sleepy TA. Unfortunately, that might be the best they got.

"I mean, it just seems so extreme, the lengths they're going to question people who were not even remotely involved," Martina was saying.

I murmured sympathetically. Apparently, Martina had spent the better part of yesterday with Detective O'Connor, going over the events of the evening Lark died.

"They even called my husband in to confirm what time he picked me up," she said, busying herself with arranging a small set of hand woodworking tools, an action that failed to cover the level of exasperation in her voice. "Not only is it ridiculous to involve him, but wouldn't any spouse lie for their partner? Not that he did, of course," she added when she saw my deer-in-the-headlights look.

"I know it's annoying, but just think of it this way: the sooner they get all this out of the way, the sooner they find the person who was actually involved," I said. "Plus, I've actually met Detective O'Connor before and he's really not so bad. I know he asks a lot of invasive questions, but he's actually a pretty reasonable person when you get down to it." I had been setting up and disentangling the cords on about a dozen drills, and looked up when I realized Martina had gone silent. She stood looking at me thoughtfully, long enough for me to remember that being besties with a police detective was not a routine matter to everyone.

"I met him last spring," I said before she could ask. "Before you got here, there was a student …" I trailed off, letting Martina fill in the blank, which she graciously did with a silent nod. It had only been about six months and I still couldn't always bring myself to say that Catherine had died.

"Anyway, all I'm saying is, you can at least know that he's a reasonable person. O'Connor may seem to get things wrong sometimes, but I definitely trust that he'll get this right in the end," I continued.

I mean, it wasn't at all true, but why let Martina worry? At the same time, I was aware of my phone lying heavily in my pocket. I might have trusted Martina completely but that didn't mean I trusted everyone around here. It was certainly worth a quick text to Arun to see if he could get any info on the alibis people were reporting.

"See, that's why I love having you around, Sam," Martina said, smiling. "That kind of attitude is what I need, especially first thing in the morning."

I returned the grin, not least because I had finally unwoven the rat's nest that happens when dozens of students dump their power tools into the same small box.

We were cut off from further conversation by the arrival of the first few students and the next hour passed quickly as we got everyone set up with their various tools. I was mercifully free to nurse my coffee in peace as the woodshop monitor came in to give the students a tutorial on the larger power tools. I only had to put it down at the sight of Martina coming over.

"Sam," she whispered. "It's so dry in here with all the sawdust, my allergies are going crazy. Could you run up to my office and grab my eye drops? It's a small bottle in the desk drawer," she asked, pressing a set of keys into my hand.

I nodded and slipped out, heading up the back stairway to the faculty offices. Martina's office wasn't hard to pick out, even if you had never been there before: It matched her bright, colorful clothes perfectly, with what looked like '70s metal office furniture over a multicolor striped rug. There was a handsome set of dark, probably cherry, shelves that she had obviously brought from home, which held a carefully curated selection of art books and the makings of a full bar. Her desk itself was surprisingly messy, the drawers a jumble of markers, paint tubes, and hot glue sticks. Luckily there was a bunch of what I assumed were the correct bottles of eye drops in the front of the drawer. I had just pocketed one when the sound of someone striding into the suite of faculty offices made me jump.

"Hi, Sam," Ricky said, coming into the doorway of Martina's office and leaning against the door frame. "I was just coming by to pick up some papers for John," she said, mentioning the art history professor she worked with. "But I'm glad I caught you."

Great. I tried not to grit my teeth too noticeably. Ricky was fine, generally, but she was the kind of person you had to be in a very particular mood to spend time with, and my wine-fogged head was definitely not in the right mood.

"I just wanted to say, I was so sorry to hear about Agnes," Ricky continued. She waited a beat, just long enough to let me ask the obvious question. I refused to give her the satisfaction, even if I was screaming the question in my head. The beat stretched uncomfortably on before Ricky continued.

"I know you two have worked really closely together," she said. "So this whole ... probably being arrested thing ... It can't be great."

No, Ricky, it wasn't great. But the last I heard, the police were just talking to Agnes. It was a leap to think that meant she had been arrested.

"Agnes is helping the police with their investigation, since she was the only person who knew Lark before he got here," I replied, trying to sound more confident than I felt. "No one said she's being arrested."

Ricky looked at me pityingly. "That's not exactly what I heard. People saw Agnes with that police detective a lot over the past couple days. And John said they were asking some of the other professors about her." I fought the urge to clutch my chest to stop my heart from beating its way out of it. The only thing that would make this conversation worse would be giving Ricky the satisfaction of having dropped devastating news on me.

"The police have to ask questions about anyone who was around during Lark's visit," I said, hating the quiver that had come into my voice. I cleared my throat to cover it. "In any event, some of us actually have a class to get back to." I pushed past her out the door.

"Okay, Sam. I just wanted to say, I'm here if you need anything. I'm sorry this is happening to you again," Ricky called after me.

I waited until I was back in the stairwell before collapsing against the wall, my hands balled into tight fists. It wasn't enough that Ricky had to make sure I knew how dire it sounded for Agnes. But for her to bring up everything that happened last semester was unforgivable. I took a few deep breaths and forced my hands to relax. At least I wasn't lying about having a class to get back to. And right about now, some loud, heavy power tools sounded like the perfect thing.

After an hour of being in a relatively small room with about a dozen students hammering away at their projects, the bustle of the lobby was a peaceful relief. I was coming out of the cafe with yet another massive coffee when I spotted Agnes at a table off to the side. It was all I could do not to sprint towards her too obviously.

"Samantha, dear. Join me?" Agnes asked as she saw me coming over.

I gratefully pulled out the chair opposite her and tried to figure out how best to ask about everything that was going on.

"It's been a rather crazy few days, hasn't it?" she said, graciously giving me the perfect opening.

"Are you okay?" I asked. "I've been hearing all kinds of crazy rumors, and I saw you with the police the other day and …" I trailed off as she reached over the table to hold my hand.

"Samantha, you absolutely do not have to worry about me, although it's very sweet that you are," Agnes said. "But you know, I've been through worse. This is just answering some questions for the police, filling in some background information."

"So no one has said anything about arresting you or …" I paused as I realized I didn't even know what the other options were for this kind of gray area, where you were the main suspect but nothing official had happened yet.

Agnes hesitated long enough for me to know everything I needed to know. "As I said, it's absolutely not something for you to worry about," she said. "I'm here now and at least we're having a lovely lunch together." We were both silent for a few minutes before she continued.

"You know, Lark wasn't always like this," Agnes said. "The way his behavior was over this visit. Believe it or not, he used to be much different. More sensitive."

I didn't say anything, willing Agnes to go on. She had such a thoughtful look on her face, as if she were a million miles or years away. I think she would have been having this same conversation silently with herself if I hadn't come over.

"We met in grad school, in Chicago," she continued. "We were both starting out, although he very quickly had success with the format he developed, the large-scale frames and structures outside." Another pause as Agnes busied herself with her salad and I waited with bated breath. "We were together, you know."

"For how long?" I asked, not wanting to cut off her flow but unable to get a hold of my curiosity.

"About eight or nine years, in all," Agnes replied with a small smile. "We lived in this tiny two-room apartment in Chicago with studio spaces a few blocks away. In those years, our whole lives were spent in the studio, only coming home late at night."

"So when did that change?" I blurted out, aware that my

curiosity had quickly veered into rudeness. Luckily, Agnes was as unfazed as ever.

"I had been offered the teaching position here in Boston. At the time, neither of us had a full-time job. We made ends meet with odd jobs – some waitressing here, some office temp work there," Agnes said. "This was a wonderful opportunity. A way to have some real stability and still be able to make work." She paused, putting her fork down with a deep sigh. "But Lark didn't want to move. He didn't want to leave his studio, his community. I didn't know it at the time, but he had already applied to the position at our alma mater in Chicago." Agnes shook her head slowly. "Nothing could change his mind. Above all else, Lark never wanted to be distracted from his work."

Before I had the chance to ask any more questions about what kind of selfish monster would choose his artwork over Agnes, we were distracted by a commotion on the other side of the lobby. We watched as Dean Winters strode across the lobby, quickly followed by an angry Martina. He turned suddenly when they were just a few feet away from us, holding up his hands at Martina in a placating gesture.

"It's just for a few weeks. A month, at most," he said. "The show will open. Just not right now."

"But any delay is ridiculous," Martina replied. I had never heard her voice reach quite the angry register she spoke in now. "The opening night was this coming Friday. Already over a week after … last week," she said, stumbling over her last words.

"But a week isn't quite enough. What would it look like if we were to have a big celebration for new faculty immediately after something like this happened?" Dean Winters shook his head. "I'm sorry, Martina, the answer is final. The show will be moved to November." He turned to go, with Martina taking a few steps after him.

"But I had press lined up already!" she called. He remained unmoved, giving a small wave at Martina over his shoulder as he continued out of the lobby and toward his office.

Martina stood frozen where she was for a few moments, visibly struggling to regain her composure. She spun on her heels, immediately spotting Agnes and me, and heading straight toward us.

"I cannot believe that man," she fumed.

I had had my own annoying run-ins with Dean Winters over the past three years, but I didn't know if he'd ever sparked a reaction this strong in anyone.

"What's going on, Martina?" Agnes asked, her face a picture of concern.

"He's moved the exhibit of new faculty work back at least a month," Martina replied, shaking her head. "After everything's been planned for weeks. We had it all set up for the opening this Friday. All the press were set to come." She threw up her hands in exasperation. "Now we're supposed to just let everything sit for weeks so the dean can make sure he looks good?" Martina made an exasperated noise, somewhere between a throat being cleared and a snarl.

I stayed silent, knowing Agnes would have the perfect gracious response. As if on cue, she replied.

"I'm sure the dean is just answering to his higher-ups," Agnes said calmly. "And there's nothing here that can't wait a few weeks. You'll still be our new faculty next month," Agnes said with a smile. Every year, the newer faculty members had a small exhibit at the start of the school year, to welcome them into the community and for us to get to know them. I was surprised that Martina felt this strongly about what was a nice but relatively minor tradition.

Martina smiled tightly. "Thank you, Agnes, I appreciate it. But it's the principle of the matter, which the dean has no respect for." With that, she gave us a curt nod and stalked off, probably heading back to her office to brood.

We were silent for a few moments. I didn't want to comment on another professor's behavior to Agnes, but wow. I hadn't seen Martina get that worked up about anything since a student suggested during a critique that the only fix for another student's work involved some overblown, five-hundred-dollar device, a comment that sent Martina into a tizzy over how art came from artists, not their tools.

As if reading my mind, Agnes spoke first. "It'll blow over," she said knowingly. "These things always do."

I nodded in agreement, silently trying to decide how to get back to the topic at hand and ask more about Lark. But Agnes was too quick for me.

"Speaking of shows here, how's your senior project going?" Agnes asked. "I seem to recall the next set of drawings was due in two weeks, correct?"

My smile faltered as I stifled a sigh. Agnes was one of my advisors for the senior project, along with Martina, and I had been successfully evading her questions for the past several weeks, about when she was going to see more of my work. In the spring, when we were supposed to set up advisors, I had proposed working on a whole miniature series about the history of pottery, working on a small scale to reproduce and play with some of the most iconic forms. I still liked the idea, and had a few design drawings to show for it, but whenever I sat down at a pottery wheel, all the energy left me.

I made a noncommittal noise. "Of course, yeah. Two weeks," I said. "I'll have the next set ready by then."

Agnes looked at me thoughtfully. "You know, Samantha, there's no rule that says you can't change your project idea. It's your project, after all," she said. "I'm just here to help."

"Thank you," I said in genuine relief. I didn't know what else I would do, but especially after everything that had happened last semester, a dry, straightforward project on art history didn't feel right.

"So, about Lark," I said, trying tactlessly to get back to the topic at hand. "I'm sorry your relationship ended like that. But … I mean," I stammered and then caught myself. I needed to come right out with it. "Is that when his behavior took a turn for the worse?"

Agnes let out a quick laugh. "It's flattering, in a way, for you to think that I could be the cause of a whole man's personality," she said as she shook her head. "But it started even before we parted ways. Lark had gotten involved in the art community in Chicago and was getting a fair amount of attention. Enough attention that it quickly went to his head." Agnes shook her head again, more sadly this time. "Lark seemed to think that he was owed some kind of fame, that he had some kind of incredible career just magically coming to him. When he realized that he couldn't even get gallery representation except for one small gallerist in Boston, well. It was just the first in a series of events that proved that, in fact, he wasn't owed anything by the world."

"But I thought he did have a long, incredible career," I replied. "It sounds like he showed all over the world. And the position in Chicago was pretty prestigious."

"True," Agnes said. "Lark had many achievements. And

you're right about his position. As the department chair, with that extensive exhibition history, he had pretty much carte blanche over what went on around campus. It was nearly a career-ending level of power."

My confusion must have shown. "Other people's careers," Agnes clarified. "Lark had final say over who was hired, who was fired. Influence over who showed at what galleries in Chicago. And he never hesitated to wield that power. But still, no matter what, it was never enough for him. Lark acted out because he could never see how much he actually had." Suddenly, all of the exhaustion and stress of the past few days were obvious on Agnes's face, in her dark undereye circles, and the lines creasing between her eyebrows.

"I'm so sorry this is happening to you," I said, reaching for her hand again. "It seems so unfair that the police have singled you out like this. I mean, I know you were the only person here that knew Lark, but still."

"Yes, although I did wonder ..." Agnes trailed off, staring thoughtfully into space for long enough that I nearly had an aneurysm trying to decide if I should say something. She shook her head quickly, shrugging off whatever the thought was. "It's no matter. I'm glad we were able to have this talk," Agnes said, patting me on the hand as she started to gather her lunch things. "Now if you'll excuse me, I still have a class to teach." She smiled, giving my arm another pat as she headed off to her afternoon class.

Knowing I needed to do the same, I checked the time on my phone. Dismayed to see that I wouldn't have time for a cigarette break first, I heaved on my backpack and headed upstairs.

Chapter 12

Friday afternoon dragged on, as it always seemed to, thoughts of that missed cigarette distracting me as our art history professor clicked through the day's slideshow. Leah, our TA and apparent best friend of Cam, the surly local artist we had met last night, sat perched at a desk in the front row, alternately taking notes and keeping a watchful eye out for those of us who might be napping in the darkened room. Or utterly distracted by their nicotine cravings and the romantic saga their mentor had just dropped on them.

As the clock ticked toward three, I couldn't hold it together any longer, my pen tapping and leg bouncing reaching a crescendo. I got up and tried to slip out of the room as unobtrusively as I could, mouthing a quick "bathroom" to Leah as I left. If I had that much nervous energy to burn, there was pretty much only one activity that would do: a little studio sleuthing.

I headed upstairs to the sculpture area, determined to find whatever evidence I could of the materials used to make all the fake "evidence" of the crime scene. Knowing the amount of paint and other materials that were used, I just couldn't see anyone hauling all the materials back out of the building unnoticed.

Upstairs, I started in the pottery studio, having already given the woodshop a quick once over during Martina's class that morning. The sculpture area was made up of half a dozen rooms: three multipurpose classrooms, the woodshop, a pottery studio with a set of wheels and two kilns that dwarfed the space, and a messy work room used for both pottery and casting that we affectionately referred to as the "Trash Can".

I had spent the most time in the pottery studio over the past few years, countless hours spent sitting at the mesmerizingly spinning wheels, churning out set after set of miniature vases, urns, and historical forms. I looked at the wheels now with an expression something like shame, aware of the work I had been neglecting.

Brushing off these feelings, I made quick work of the pottery studio, peeking behind the kiln, under tables, pushing aside bottles and buckets of glaze. Nothing jumped out at me as anything that shouldn't be there. I knew the room well enough to know that nothing much had changed over the past week or two.

I entered the connecting door to the Trash Can, overwhelmed as I always was by the sight and smell of this many art materials in one place. I often had the urge to reach for lab goggles and a ventilator in this room, even if nothing was toxic (or particularly toxic). The messy work benches and the shelves lining the room were covered with buckets of plaster, concrete and clay, small baskets with a million different hand tools, and about a decade's worth of student molds in rubber and plastic. The piece de resistance was the shop sink, a cast-iron behemoth caked in decades of plaster and glazes, such that you could only see the faint outline of the actual sink beneath this hardened exterior.

Luckily, I had come in during a rare moment when no one was working in the room. I guess I wasn't the only one who would rather be anywhere else but school on a Friday afternoon. I got to work on the obvious hiding places first, peering under the tables and using a yardstick to open the door of a metal cabinet that held the actually toxic materials (and not for the first time, I wondered how much more dangerous all these old bottles of shellac and oil-based varnishes got the longer they sat there).

Not finding anything suspicious (although you could reasonably project suspicion onto pretty much any of the student work-in-progresses in the room), I donned a mask and goggles before I started in on the shelves, even snapping on a pair of rubber gloves. Overkill? Probably, but I had also eaten enough plaster dust over the years to know that I didn't want to inhale any more than I had to.

I got up on a chair to rummage through the various buckets and bottles on the shelves, not finding anything of interest until the third shelf, where a gallon of red paint caught my eye. It wasn't the paint that was unusual, since this can was on a shelf with another ten cans of paint. But this can looked brand new, its shiny white label sporting only a few rusty drops of blood - I mean paint - but not yet covered by a few years' worth of dust and grime. I checked the label on the lid, noting the date it was mixed by a hardware store: about three weeks ago. Unfortunately, that was all the information I had to go on. I snapped a quick photo of the paint and slid it back to where it was on the back of the shelf.

After the high of this discovery, the next ten minutes passed by uneventfully as I checked the next few sets of shelves. The monotonous task had me slipping off into a daydream about what I was going to eat for dinner, until the sound of the door slamming open rudely jarred me back to earth.

"Oh, uh. I didn't realize someone was in here." We looked at each other in surprise. I was suddenly and crushingly aware of what I looked like in my makeshift hazmat suit. The mask in particular had a lovely way of clamping down on certain sections of my curly hair, creating a gorgeous poodle effect.

"Charles, right?" I asked, taking off the mask as quickly as I could and patting my hair back into shape. "I'm Sam."

"Uh, yeah. Charles," he stammered. He did indeed look like a younger Paul Rudd, albeit one who was currently crossed with a deer caught in headlights.

"It's fine if you want to come work in here," I said, with what I hoped was a welcoming smile. I didn't know Charles well at all, except for the fact that he was the performance student whom Lark had recently embarrassed during a crit. "I was just finishing up."

"No, it's cool," Charles replied, slowly backing out of the door. "I'll come back later. I, uh. Forgot something in my locker." I barely heard the last part of that sentence, as he had practically been running down the hallway already. I rolled my eyes at how overblown Mel's comments must have been. He seemed about a million miles away from the cocky, angry guy Mel had described.

I was still standing on the chair and had been holding a cardboard box full of scraps throughout this exchange. I was about to put it back on the shelf when I realized with a jolt what I was looking at: a box full of fabric scraps, most with at least one edge unraveled, creating small bundles of threads. My breath caught as I sifted through the heap, seeing a turquoise fabric identical to the pile of threads I had first seen in the classroom when I found Lark.

So this was the smoking gun, as it were. If there was any doubt about the authenticity of the crime scene, this box alone could blow it out of the water. And I was holding this box when Charles, someone apparently cocky and confident enough to fight with a world-famous visiting artist, was suddenly so nervous he had to basically flee the scene.

I took a few pictures of the contents of the box before replacing it to the shelf. Whether it belonged to Charles or someone else, I didn't exactly want anyone to know that I knew about it, and made sure it was replaced in exactly the same position it had been in. As I was doing so, another question came to mind: Other than retrieving this box, what believable excuse did a performance art student have for being in the sculpture area?

I was saying as much to the crowd around the dinner table just a few hours later. Stephanie and Arun had come over to our place after work, bringing with them tubs of their mother's chicken curry, which the five of us (since Mel had once again wormed her way into dinner with Rebecca and I) were currently making quick work of. I paused long enough to wipe an errant drip of the coconut milk sauce off my chin, knowing the curry would still leave an incriminating stain. Sita seemed to have an innate knowledge of just how much spicy curry could be tempered by this exact amount of coconut milk, a knowledge that was the only reason the fiery bowl wasn't burning off my taste buds. Or at least not all of them.

Mel took my pause as an opportunity to leap in. "To give him the benefit of the doubt, Charles's performances do involve a fair amount of sculpture," she said. "Remember? That was the whole issue with Lark in the first place. Sculpture was for sculptors and performance art was for … well, crazy kids was the gist of it as far as I heard."

"Even so, the performance area has rooms available for students to work in," I argued. "Unless there was a specific tool he needed, there's no real reason he couldn't have worked in the performance area."

We continued pointlessly in this vein for a few minutes before Arun cut in. "I hate to break up this inter-departmental squabble, but I had another phone call with the police press office today that you might want to hear about." He waited until we nodded our assent, Mel adding a sassy head shake that seemed to say she'd have been proven right if allowed to continue. "The press officer provided only a couple of updates," Arun started. "First, they think he was killed sometime between six and eight pm. Most people left the reception around six, so for a lot of people, their alibi is that they were on their way home. A lot of people drove themselves home alone and since no one ever remembers a random person they saw on the subway, the police can't exactly verify most of these alibis." Arun paused, then continued quickly enough to cut off Mel from interrupting again. "I'm afraid that Agnes is one of these people," Arun said, turning to look at me directly. "She drove herself home and spent the evening alone. There's apparently one phone call to a sister that was made from her landline, but it was late enough to be just outside the window when Lark was killed."

"Who even has a landline anymore?" Mel asked obliviously, which we all ignored.

"Martina is just about the only person with a confirmed alibi, since her husband came by the school to pick her up," Arun continued. "So I'm sorry not to have better news." I nodded my thanks.

"What about CCTV?" Rebecca asked. "The security cameras from school?"

I groaned. The lax security force was a much-loved topic of griping around school. Students and staff alike never ceased to enjoy complaining about security's ability to ignore major rule infringements like smoking pot inside, while they berated students for simple things like a forgotten ID card.

"I did ask about that," Arun replied. "But there were so many people coming and going, it's basically meaningless."

"That makes sense," I said. "A lot of people stay after class to work, so it wouldn't have been weird for anyone to be in the building late on a weeknight."

We ate in silence for a few moments, digesting this lack of groundbreaking information.

"Did you find out anything else new?" Rebecca asked hopefully.

"I did hear a bit more about the cause of death," Arun said. "Apparently, they've narrowed it down enough to know that the poison was some kind of vasoconstrictor." Arun then went off on a long tangent about the pharmacodynamics of this term, most of which was above my paygrade.

"Basically, it was something that narrowed all the arteries in his body so that blood couldn't get to major organs and he died?" I cut in, getting the side eye from Arun. I loved him, but he did have a tendency toward lengthy explanations. Which I guess at least gave his editor something to do.

"Yeah, that's pretty much the gist of it," he replied. "Identifying a specific rare poison is a bit beyond the usual police lab's capacity, since the press officer made it sound like there were about a thousand different possibilities. They're sending it out to another state lab who can do more extensive testing."

"Which will tell us what, exactly?" Steph asked. "We know that Lark was poisoned already."

The rest of us were silent for a beat. "Thanks, Debbie downer," I said, kicking her (gently) under the table. "Everything counts. You never know what may be our big break here."

Arun nodded. "Plus, it sounds like you have a lot of plans for the weekend?" he asked me.

It was my turn to nod. "We're gonna go check out Cam's workplace venture," I said, gesturing to Rebecca, who had agreed to go with me.

"You know, there's also a performance this weekend. Charles is in it," Mel said. "Our whole class is, kind of. I mean, I'm not doing anything," she said as if the thought were outrageous. "But a few of the people in class are also in the same performance class, and they're having some kind of show. Tomorrow afternoon."

I looked across the table at Stephanie, who was busying herself with the last of the curry. "How'd you feel about seeing your first performance art show?" I asked her.

Steph looked up mid-bite, snorting when she realized whom I was asking. "No thanks," she said. "I have, uh. Anything else to do."

"Come on, it would be good for you," Arun said. "Broaden your horizons. Or at least give you something to laugh about. Either way, you should go. I'm out on assignment most of the weekend, or I'd go." Arun was stuck covering a huge sailing regatta that happened on the Charles River every fall, which meant he would have to spend most of the weekend learning what all those sailing terms actually meant.

"Fine," Steph said with an eye roll. "But I swear, the first person to take off their clothes or ask for audience volunteers, I'm out of there."

"Fair enough. I won't volunteer to take off my clothes too soon, then," I said, receiving a glare for my sins.

Chapter 13

I woke up the next morning to the smell of toast and coffee, the sounds of pans clanging around as breakfast was being made. I threw on an oversized sweatshirt over my pajamas and padded down the hall in search of coffee. Rebecca was in the kitchen, humming along to the radio as she whisked a bowl of eggs, hovering over a pan of sizzling butter.

"Two scrambled?" she asked, gesturing to the bowl.

I nodded gratefully, still asleep enough that I couldn't quite make the appropriate noises yet.

In a matter of minutes, I was ensconced at the table in front of a steaming plate of eggs and toast, a brimming cup of coffee in hand. There were much, much worse ways to start a day.

Rebecca slid into the chair across from me. "I didn't get a chance to tell you last night," she started, "but I did have coffee with Tia yesterday, that girl from the gallery next to mine?" I nodded, even managing a small murmur between bites of toast.

"She said that it was pretty much an open secret that Lark was trying to leave Giulia," Rebecca said, gesturing with her fork in punctuation. "Apparently he didn't make any attempt to go about it quietly. Lark was asking anyone and everyone if they knew someone taking on new artists who would be interested." I snorted at this. Who would've thought, Lark acting with disregard for professional mores and people's feelings?

"Also, the other rumors were true too," Rebecca continued. "About Giulia's money issues. Tia said her boss, Peter Harrison, had lunch with Giulia last week and came back looking all concerned – which was really barely disguised glee." We both rolled our eyes. In pretty much any other sector, it seemed small business owners were good at banding together and supporting one another. But art dealers appeared to be overall a pretty merciless bunch.

"She told Peter that if they didn't have a spectacularly good month, she would have to close in the next few weeks," Rebecca said. "I don't know what the issue is, exactly, other than just not selling enough. If Lark hadn't died …" She trailed off as we both realized the implication of this thought, which was enough to finally jolt me more awake.

"Giulia would have closed without the sales after his death," I finished the thought, rubbing the last of the sleep from my eyes.

"I mean, we don't actually know that Lark's work is selling a lot right now," Rebecca reasoned. "We're just assuming based on the fact that his work will almost definitely go up in value." I guess she was right, but it seemed like an extremely safe assumption for us to be making.

"Well, it seems fair then that we should pay Giulia another visit," I said. "Just to confirm our thinking. You up for a little gallery hopping tomorrow?"

Rebecca nodded, trying too late to disguise her eagerness. I grinned behind my coffee. It was nice to see that Rebecca was finally coming around on all this sleuthing business. I needed a good partner in crime.

And luckily, I had one for my next errand. Steph and I had arranged to meet at Cam's workspace venture at eleven, and as always, she was already waiting out front when I ran up to the building a few minutes late. Okay, fifteen minutes late – but I did text to warn her. Steph just rolled her eyes in greeting, no longer bothering to scold me for my bad habits. I offered an apologetic wheeze as I struggled to catch my breath.

"So," I said as soon as I could speak again. "You don't mind visiting a 'collaborative workspace venture' but you're skeptical of a performance art show?"

Steph shrugged. "This is just a building, it's somebody's business. How obnoxious could it be?"

I gave her a knowing grin. Reasonable, but only to anyone who hasn't been in an "artist-designed space" before.

We clattered up the noisy, industrial metal stairs inside the building to the second floor, as directed by new chrome signs that looked recently affixed to the brick walls. The building was a huge old industrial workspace in an area of Boston where most such buildings had already been transformed into condos or fancy restaurants or both. I marveled at Cam's ability to find a building like this still standing, untouched.

At the sound of the door creaking open on the second floor, all eyes turned toward us as we took in the space and the sight of the work crew. I could just make out Cam in the dusty gloom, who stood across the room and was in the middle of barking orders from a short step ladder at another man on a much larger ladder, both of whom were gesturing up at the ceiling. Before I could get further absorbed in whatever drama was unfolding there, Leah came bounding over to us.

"Hi Sam! I'm so glad you guys could stop by!"

I was glad we had picked eleven am to come over; any earlier and Leah's perky energy would have too much for me to take.

She waited expectantly for me to introduce Stephanie, who promptly dialed the charm way up.

"I'm so glad we could," Steph gushed. "This looks like an incredible space! I'd love to get the tour."

Leah beamed. "Are you an artist also?" she asked.

"Yes, thanks for asking. I do mostly photography. Black-and-white, old school, you know. Stuff like that."

I stifled a snort at Steph's reply.

"Oh, that's great. We're going to put in a small darkroom just over there," Leah said, gesturing vaguely at the back wall. "And there'll be a digital studio as well, for photo editing and everything." She paused long enough for us to murmur in appreciation, and I wondered at her level of pride. I realized I didn't know exactly what her role was here, beyond being some kind of wrangler for Cam, and asked as much.

"Oh, I do a little of this and a little of that," Leah answered vaguely. "It's really a passion project for Cam. I just help out on the weekends mostly. Provide extra support for the crew, help with some of the design work." Leah looked around, waving and calling for Cam to come over. "I could give you the tour, but Cam's the one who really has the big picture."

Cam ambled over, not bothering to hide his frustration at being called away from his work. I marveled again at the idea of sweet, upbeat Leah being with this sulky man.

"What's up, Leah?" Cam asked curtly in greeting.

"These ladies are artists from school," Leah said. We didn't bother to correct her mistaking Steph for a student. If Steph wanted to be a photo student for the day, it was fine by me. "They were interested in touring the space. I think you mentioned maybe needing studio space after graduating this year?"

"That's right," I said, nodding vigorously. "We're already worrying about where we'll be able to work next year, what with the price of studio space being crazy around here." Sometimes the only way to deal with people like Cam was to lay it on as thickly as possible. "And then Leah was telling us about your space, which sounded just incredible. So we'd love to get a tour. If that's possible at all." I was proud at how perfectly I was nailing this mix of flattery.

Cam did seem to soften, at least a bit. Or to whatever extent counted as soft for Cam. "Sure, I can show you around," he agreed. "It's not just studio spaces, actually. There'll be a suite of different workspaces, both ones to provide specific tools and breakout areas to foster interdisciplinary dialogue."

I should have warned Steph in advance about Cam's language, then reasoned that she should be pretty fairly warned by the very fact that she was coming to a "collaborative workspace venture."

"Oh, that sounds awesome," Steph was saying, in as genuine a voice as she could muster.

"Yeah, we believe that there's no real point in just giving people access to tools and everything if you don't also provide spaces where real collaboration can occur," Cam said in the most earnest voice I had heard him use. "This front zone we're standing in now is the welcome area, where artists can sign in and out, see what events are going on here, and sign up for the different studio spaces."

He moved farther into the space, gesturing to his right and left as we followed him. "This area will be a woodshop, complete with CNC router and laser cutter. And next to it is a digital sculpture space, with 3D printing capabilities." I bristled at his use of the term "digital sculpture," but reminded myself that we were here to investigate, not bicker over art terms that would probably go out of vogue tomorrow anyway.

"This whole zone here," Cam said, drawing a circle with his arms that encompassed the entire middle of the room, "will be for artist studio spaces. We're setting it up so that between every two or three studios, there's an open common area, even if it's just a sofa or a couple of chairs. So we're really building in these collaborative innovation zones right into the studio model." Sure, that was one way to think about a couple of chairs.

I didn't ask how artists were supposed to get any work done when people were hanging out right outside their studio, instead remarking on the progress of the space. "This all sounds amazing, but it looks like you guys have quite a way to go," I said while feigning concern over my future studio space. "Do you think it'll be ready if we want to rent in the spring?"

Cam's grimace returned, and Leah placed a preemptively placating hand on his arm. "We'll be ready by the spring," he said determinedly.

"I'm sorry, Lark's death must have really caused some setbacks for you," I said with sympathy. "I know you two were business partners." I wouldn't have thought that Cam's grimace could get much darker, but I was definitely wrong.

"Lark never did anything," Cam spat out. "His death isn't a problem for our progress." I could see Leah's grip tighten on his arm. I'd be worried, too, if I wanted to prevent Cam from speaking ill of the dead (instead of wanting to goad him into it, which was my real motivation).

"Got it – kind of shadow partner?" Steph asked.

"If you could even call it that," Cam answered.

Leah cut him off before he could say anything else. "Cam, I don't think the girls need to hear about Lark's behavior. As you said, it doesn't affect the timeline for the studios."

"No, people should know what kind of person he was really like," Cam said and shook off Leah's grip. "Lark loved the idea here. He was really into it at first and volunteered to help us get our first round of seed money, even promising an investment of his own. But then, it was like Lark thought his very presence was enough. Like he was such a big man he didn't need to put in any actual work."

"So you weren't able to get the funding?" I asked.

"We were, but nowhere near as much as we would have been able to get if we'd had more than just Lark's name involved," Cam answered. "And that personal investment? It was always in the mail."

Steph and I nodded in understanding while Leah forcibly turned our attention back to the tour. As we were shown through the roughly framed spaces where a future darkroom, video editing suite and sound recording studio would be, I thought about the sheer force of Cam's anger. So Lark had promised him money and commitment, then left him high and dry on both counts. But I still couldn't see how Lark's death would benefit Cam, exactly. It's not like he would ever get the money now.

I said as much to Stephanie as soon as we had made our way back outside, blinking in the bright sunlight after the gloom and industrial lights inside.

"But if Cam were that angry, then killing Lark itself would be the benefit. You know, it's revenge," Steph added when she saw the look I was giving her. "What? I'm not saying that I would feel great about killing someone I'm angry at. I'm just saying, it definitely could be true for Cam."

"Great, glad to hear you're only good at *thinking* of motives for murder," I said as I threaded my arm through hers. I glanced at the time on my phone, seeing that we had made it out of the land of innovative collaboration at noon on the dot. "And how good are you at thinking of places for lunch?"

We spent the afternoon killing time before the four pm performance show, mostly by hopping from one thrift store to the next. It was funny how, on the surface, it might have looked like any other day on the town, when in reality, we were investigating a murder the whole time. (Okay, maybe not when I was trying on vintage dresses. Unless that counted as buying disguises.)

Once we got to school, I was surprised that Steph actually walked in on her own without me having to literally drag her, since she had spent the afternoon speculating about what kinds of horrible performances she might have to see. I was afraid her suspicions would be confirmed when we turned down the hall to the performance area and were enveloped by a cacophony of noises.

When I realized what I was hearing, I stopped in my tracks, suddenly hearing the answer to a question that had been nagging at me all week. How had someone made such a huge mess in the room where Lark was killed without anyone else noticing? I couldn't think of a single way a table got flipped silently.

Steph got a few steps ahead of me before she realized I had stopped. "Sam, come on," she said, clearly ready to complain again about my dragging her down here, but I held up my hand to cut her off. It wasn't what I heard that was remarkable. It sounded like a dozen kittens crying out while they scaled their way noisily up the side of a building, so nothing out of the ordinary for the performance area. But it was the fact that I heard anything at all. Suddenly, the scene in the classroom when Lark was killed made a whole lot more sense. I would have to check the class schedule to see who met here Monday nights, but I was pretty sure that whoever it was would have been making such a racket that – just down the hall from where we stood now – no one would have ever heard or guessed what was going on, leaving our murderer free to flip tables and throw chairs around in peace.

I explained this to Steph in a hurried whisper as we walked into the performance studio, slipping into two chairs in the back row, where I figured Steph would be safest from anyone asking for audience volunteers.

"They should have called it *Ten-minute Torture,*" Steph said when she saw the title on the program, *Five-minute Freestyle.*

"Oh, come on. You haven't even seen anything yet …" I elbowed her. "You could be surprised."

Steph made a face that left no doubt as to what she thought about that prospect.

According to the program, Charles was third in the lineup. As the first performer finished their five minutes with a series of screams, I was almost inclined to agree with Stephanie about her title suggestion.

At least Charles's five minutes started inauspiciously enough, as he carried out stack after stack of plain white dinner plates. I could tell, even from the back row, that these plates were hand thrown and unfinished in a way that you'd never be able to buy. I silently revised my list of reasons that a performance art student could plausibly be in the sculpture area and was just about to whisper about my newly lenient attitude to Steph when I heard the first crash.

Charles proceeded to spend the rest of his five minutes smashing his way through the stacks of dinner plates. He alternated his rhythm, throwing plates against the wall quickly with both hands, then dropping them slowly one by one onto the floor. I didn't risk a glance at Stephanie, who I was sure was currently rolling her eyes so hard I could practically hear it.

As soon as Charles's five minutes were up and he had swept the front of the room clean again, I grabbed Steph's arm and nodded my head towards the door. We didn't speak until we got outside.

"Well, he definitely has some, uh …" I stammered, unsure how to translate the very clear picture in my head. The scene after Charles's performance was practically identical to the room, I had found Lark in, albeit with more white pottery and less red paint.

"Issues? Anger?" Steph volunteered.

"Anger," I agreed. "He's definitely a person with some anger to work out." A lot of anger to work out. And I could only wonder what else he might have taken his anger out on.

Chapter 14

Stephanie was spared any further art atrocities the next day, since Rebecca had already agreed to a second visit to Giulia's gallery with me. Not that I expected any performance or other art-related indignities at a blue-chip gallery like Giulia's, but I guess you never know.

Rebecca and I arrived around eleven just a few minutes after the gallery opened, ensuring we were the only people there. We milled around awkwardly for a few minutes, pretending to be absorbed in Lark's photographs, which still hung throughout the gallery. Rebecca casually elbowed me, tilting her head toward the reception desk. We had agreed on the way over that the gallery assistant would be a good source of information, likely to open up to another intern like Rebecca. And lucky for me, the woman at the desk today wasn't the one who had caught me in Giulia's office the other day.

"Everything in here looks beautiful," Rebecca gushed as we took the few steps across the small space to the reception desk. "All the photos really look great in this space."

The assistant nodded graciously, smiling. "Thank you. There's an exhibit guide here, if you'd like," she said, offering each of us a small brochure. It had one of Lark's iconic works on the front: a red powder-coated steel frame in a large arch that held a sheet of corrugated, wavy plexiglass. I nodded and murmured in what I hoped was an appreciative tone. There was just something about galleries like this that brought out the crankiest side of me, which is why I'd readily agreed when Rebecca had suggested that she would do most of the talking.

"Oh, this is great, thank you," Rebecca said as she flipped through the small pamphlet. She was so used to this atmosphere that I noticed her eyes didn't even widen as she scanned some of the prices. Giulia was asking a cool million for that red steel and plexi piece and the crazy thing was, I thought even this price might be low. I mean, the man just died. If ever there was a time to exploit the market, it was probably now. See? This is why I had promised to keep my mouth shut today.

"I think it's great the photos were printed so large. This way they really fill up the space. You know, take up the space they're meant to have," Rebecca was saying as she gestured to the photos on the wall opposite us. "It's a pretty big space compared to some of the galleries around here," she continued. "It must be really expensive to rent."

The gallery assistant's eyes widened at this last remark. Even I was surprised that Rebecca just went for it like that. This was not really an industry where transparency around prices, whether of artwork or rent, was usually valued.

"I mean, I know for our gallery, Betsy Gilbert? I intern there," Rebecca rushed on before the assistant's eyes could get any wider. "Betsy's always complaining about the rent on this block. She says the galleries here are way more expensive than those gallery spaces on the waterfront downtown."

At the news of another struggling gallery owner, the assistant seemed to perk up a bit. "It's true," she commiserated, "Giulia complains about the rent all the time. They may even raise it again at the start of next year."

"That's awful …" Rebecca shook her head as if this was news to her, and not something Betsy had told her weeks before. Of course, Betsy had thrown in a few extra choice words about the owners that the assistant had skipped, but. The news was the same.

"Giulia must have to sell a really high volume each month, then. At least these look like they've been selling pretty well," Rebecca said with another vague gesture at the photos where there was a smattering of red dots on the wall labels, signaling a sale. The uneasiness returned to the assistant's face and she even visibly squirmed in her chair, as if she were allergic to talking about money.

"Giulia does what she can," the assistant said eventually. "As I'm sure Betsy does as well. Giulia has even been looking into some alternative spaces recently." The assistant instantly looked like she wished she could take back her last comment. "Alternative spaces" was a pretty damning remark, if I knew anything about the way gallerists spoke: it was basically code for closing, or at least for whatever the last stage was right before closing.

"Oh, of course," Rebecca said while vigorously nodding. "And even Betsy talks about closing at least once a month. I mean, I'm pretty sure she's just being dramatic, but still. I know that's always a problem for small galleries like ours." Rebecca's mouth was still open, poised to ask another question the poor assistant clearly did not want to answer, when an office door closed in the background and the woman herself swept into the gallery space.

"Tell them it won't be a problem," Giulia was saying in her heavily inflected Italian accent.

At first, I thought she was speaking to the room at large, before I clocked the small Bluetooth headset she was wearing.

"I'm going out for my eleven-thirty," she called to the assistant as she flung a huge black pashmina over her shoulder. The assistant had stood up the second Giulia came into the room and continued to stand there, nodding like a bobble head, even after the heavy glass doors had clicked shut again.

"Well, the photos are great. Thanks for the exhibit guide," Rebecca said, freeing the assistant from our awkward attention. The two of us returned to aimlessly milling around, making quiet comments to each other as if truly in awe of the photos.

"How about getting some coffee?" I asked Rebecca as we finished up our circuit of the room. "I know a great place nearby."

She agreed, and we left the gallery with a small wave to the assistant, stepping out into the kind of October day that's too warm in the sun and freezing cold in the shade. From our vantage point in front of the gallery, I watched as Giulia waited at the corner before crossing the street and making a right turn.

"The coffee shop I know is that way," I said, with a gesture in the same general direction that Giulia had just gone.

"Great!" Rebecca said. "Is it pretty close? I could really use something sweet right about now."

"Yeah, yeah. It's, uh. Pretty close." I hurried us to the corner and craned my neck to see down the street. Thank god Giulia was so tall: I could still see her bouffant from nearly a block away as she bobbed down the street. "It's just this way."

I threaded my arm through Rebecca's with a shiver, as if I were just hoping to keep warm on the shady side of the street, and not like I was hoping to pull her along with me quickly. Rebecca made small talk as we walked along, chatting about this class and that student, who had done what for which assignment due tomorrow. I kept my eyes ahead, trained on Giulia, and abruptly brought us up short when I saw her duck into a doorway.

"I, uh, just need to check the directions on my phone," I said, hoping that whatever Giulia was doing inside would be quick. I was famously bad with directions, but even I couldn't believably look for a nearby coffee shop for an hour. From the corner of my eye, it looked like Giulia had gone into a bank ATM, and she reemerged a few minutes later. I breathed a sigh of relief, dropping my phone back into my pocket and marching confidently ahead. "It's this way, I was right the first time." Rebecca shrugged in acceptance, and we continued on ahead.

We followed Giulia for the next few blocks, as I kept a careful hand on Rebecca's arm, slowing us down and speeding us up as needed so that we stayed a reasonable distance behind Giulia. I mean, not that I'd ever followed anyone before or had any idea what I was doing, but thirty feet or so seemed to match what I'd seen in movies, so that was good enough for me.

Giulia crossed the street ahead of us as we got caught at the intersection. I nodded along to what Rebecca was saying about the other students in her papermaking class as I watched Giulia confidently cross again at the other side of the street, walking up the front steps of a building on the next block, across from our side of the street. I scanned the shops, wildly hoping that there would be a miraculously great coffee shop with clear sight lines of Giulia.

"That's it, actually," I said, pointing to the sign of the first coffee place I spotted.

"A Starbucks?" Rebecca asked. "Your great coffee shop is a Starbucks?"

"Uh, yep. It's a Starbucks." I tried not to sound surprised. "There's not really anything else worth going to close to the galleries."

Mercifully, Rebecca just shrugged. "Okay, whatever. I just need some coffee, wherever it comes from."

I was relieved enough to pay for both our coffees, throwing in a few croissants in case we needed an excuse to stay awhile. The building Giulia had gone into was an old townhouse, of the kind that had mostly been converted to offices in this neighborhood. Whatever her eleven-thirty appointment was, it was at a pretty toney office.

"So, what do you think Giulia is doing?" Rebecca asked as soon as we were ensconced at a table near the front window. I froze. Obviously, I had been found out, but I wasn't sure yet the extent of the lie I had caught myself in. Rebecca blew on her coffee, oblivious to my discomfort.

"Um, I have no idea?" I winced. Rebecca knew I only up-talked when I was lying.

"Well, it's a pretty fancy office building she went to for her meeting. Maybe a private bank? Or a fancy doctor?" Rebecca tore into one of the croissants, still refusing to meet my eye, pretending to be absorbed in the mediocre pastry. When she finally looked up, Rebecca started to giggle at the sight of the anxious expression on my face.

"What, did you think I really didn't know? You practically dragged me down the street after her," Rebecca said. She continued to laugh as if being forced on a stakeout was the funniest thing to have ever happened to her. "I mean, you literally grabbed my arm the whole way," she said, gasping for breath between laughs as she mimed pulling someone along.

"I ... I didn't realize you knew," I stammered. "I'm sorry, I just didn't think you'd … You know. Be okay with following someone like that."

Once she'd sufficiently recovered, Rebecca shrugged. "Giulia is a pretty strong suspect, as far I'm concerned. She was definitely struggling and probably going to close, if she was looking into alternative spaces," Rebecca said, putting air quotes around "alternative spaces." "Plus, what she said on the phone as she was leaving? Didn't exactly sound like an innocent remark."

"It's true, it was almost *too* obviously suspicious," I said. "Maybe it had nothing to do with her gallery or the money. But who do you think she was talking to?"

"No idea." Rebecca shook her head. "All I know is, for her to be talking about her money issues to a lowly gallery assistant means it must be pretty serious."

"Or it was pretty serious," I pointed out. "It looked like a fair amount of those photos had sold." I paused as I realized how crass it felt to be talking about work selling at what had felt like a memorial event just a few days before.

Before Rebecca had a chance to respond, I shushed her, nodding across the street to where Giulia was coming out of the office building. She turned left, heading back in the direction we had come from.

Rebecca checked the time. "Thirty minutes," she said. "I don't know if that's an appointment that went really well, or if that's a bad sign."

We gathered up our things quickly, waiting impatiently at the corner to cross over to the office building. There was a small brass plaque above the doorbell, with three names engraved on it.

"It looks like a lawyer's office," I said, tilting my phone screen so Rebecca could see the search results. "Daniel Leonhardt, estate planning services," I read off the firm's website. "Wills, trusts, estate administration." I looked at Rebecca in confusion. "But why would Giulia be here? I'm sure Lark has some kind of family, somewhere, who would be taking care of this kind of thing."

"Maybe. But it's possible this isn't personal." Rebecca looked thoughtful. "I remember the day after Lark died, Betsy was talking about this artist she used to represent, who passed away a few years ago. Just of old age, natural causes. And even then, she said it was a nightmare trying to get through probate and get ahold of the remaining artwork, which belonged to Betsy under the terms of their contract."

"So Giulia may be trying to get the rest of Lark's work?" I asked. "Whatever she doesn't already own or have in storage?"

"Exactly," Rebecca nodded. "I can't think of why else she'd need an estate attorney right now."

We stood silently for a few moments, both of us mulling this new information over, until my phone started to go off. It was a text from Arun, asking how it was going at the gallery. How was it going?

Well, I wasn't sure how he'd react to our following a murder suspect. But I certainly had a lot to tell him.

We settled on a picnic dinner at the Arnold Arboretum, a huge expanse of trees, flowers, and rolling green hills that was lush enough to make you forget that you were still in the middle of Boston. Arun had finished his assignment for the day, and groaned when I asked how the regatta had been.

"Please don't say the words 'crew,' 'boat,' or 'Charles' to me for the rest of the day," he replied.

"That good, huh?" I grinned. The regatta was always a huge mess of people, a cacophony of air horns and cheers.

Arun shook his head. "Talk to me about anything else," he begged. "What happened at Giulia's gallery?"

I gave him the summary of our talk with the gallery assistant, then tried to gloss over us following her as I told Arun about the meeting with the lawyer. Other than a brief warning look, I was spared any choice words about our tailing Giulia.

"That must have been a pretty expensive meeting, if she paid for a Sunday appointment," Arun said. "That's gotta be something pretty important to her."

I had to agree that Giulia was looking more and more like our prime suspect. But there was something that had been niggling at me all afternoon.

"But the problem with Giulia as a suspect is that she's such a theatrical woman," I said. "So she would definitely be capable of – maybe even likely to – create a scene like the one I found Lark in. But that same theatricality means that it would have been hard for her not to stand out at school." There weren't that many six-foot-tall Italian women swanning around the building in head-to-toe designer clothes, after all. No matter how lax our security was, I doubt she would have gone unnoticed.

"Plus," I added, "she would have had to bring in all the materials for the faux evidence. Making it all the more likely that she would have been noticed and somebody would remember seeing her." I pictured Giulia, dressed as she had been today into a long black ensemble punctuated by high-heeled boots that pushed her past six feet, walking around the department building dragging shopping bags of paint and fabric with her.

"I just don't see it," I said with a sigh. "I hate to admit it. She's our best suspect. Our best hope for …" I trailed off. I still couldn't bring myself to admit the degree of danger that Agnes might be in at that moment, how much she needed us to help redirect the police.

Arun put his arm around me, squeezing me close. "I know you're worried about Agnes," he said. "And we are helping her, I promise. But it doesn't help to give the police an unlikely suspect."

I nodded, hoping what he said was true. It was a fine balance of wishing someone else to be the actual killer and not wanting to make wild accusations against innocent people.

"Well," I said with a sigh, "at least she's not the only person we learned a bit more about this weekend." I gave Arun the rundown on our visit to Cam's space, although I was pretty sure Steph had already regaled him with all the ridiculous vocab Cam used.

"He's just … odd," I finished.

"I don't think Cam is a particularly strong suspect," Arun said, hugging me tightly again when he saw my face start to fall. "It's just not obvious how he would benefit from Lark's death. If Cam wasn't getting any money before, he's definitely not getting Lark's money now."

"True, but you never really know how someone will act when they're in a complete rage," I said.

"Which sounds pretty much the same as what Stephanie came home saying last night," Arun replied. I grinned, thinking of what she must have said about the performance show. "But I still come back to this with Charles: Would you really kill someone over one bad crit?"

My brain might have said yes since, as with Cam, you never

really knew what could happen when the red mist descended for someone. But my gut said no, and I said as much to Arun.

"It was too small a slight to cause an act like this," I reasoned. "If Lark were a professor, who was repeating things like that to Charles on a daily basis, then maybe Charles would respond strongly. But as a visiting artist, Lark would have been gone soon anyway …" I trailed off as I realized what this meant.

"Which really means that for whoever killed him, it wasn't enough that Lark just leave Boston," I went on hurriedly. "And that means that maybe whoever killed him wasn't in Boston at all." I looked up, almost laughing when I saw how adorably confused Arun looked at my admittedly confusing thought.

"What I mean is, so far we've only looked at the people who are in Boston or tied to Lark's work here in Boston. But he's an older man with a long career; there must be a million people waiting in the wings who would be a part of his story." I mean, I hoped there weren't a million. But a few people, if at least one of them could neatly redirect attention away from Agnes, would be great.

"Yep, that makes a lot more sense than a murderer working remotely," Arun said with a grin. "I can do some digging into Lark's past at work tomorrow. I'm still working on a 'profile' of him, after all," Arun said with air quotes. "I think that makes a little archival research necessary."

I smiled, leaning on my head on his shoulder, content to leave behind all talk of investigating and artists for now. "If I don't say 'boat' or 'regatta' to you, you have to promise not to say 'artist' or 'suspect' or 'murder' to me."

"Deal," he said. At least for now.

Chapter 15

I woke up in the middle of the night on Sunday in a cold sweat, bathed in the blue light of my laptop, which continued playing a *Murder She Wrote* marathon even though I had fallen asleep hours ago. Despite my inauspicious surroundings, I was jolted wide awake by a sudden realization: This whole time, we'd been assuming that Lark casually stayed behind at school after his artist's talk, with someone who was already in the building or had gone to the talk. But what if he had been planning to meet someone all along?

As I half-heartedly watched Angela Lansbury sweep through Cabot Cove on her latest investigation, I wondered how we'd ever be able to figure out who, if anyone, Lark had been planning to meet. We'd never get access to his phone, which was presumably stored in some police evidence lockup downtown. But there might be a planner or a notebook with his things, anything that might show an appointment Lark had scheduled for the night he'd been killed. And luckily, since I was the one who helped Martina book the apartment rentals for each visiting artist, I knew exactly where those things were. Even though it was nearly one in the morning, I texted the one person I knew who wouldn't say no to some light breaking and entering.

Steph and I met a few blocks from where Lark was staying first thing in the morning, because I couldn't think of a less suspicious time than Monday morning. Monday mornings were for a quick cup of coffee while you hustled back into the office and got down to work. Most people didn't take time on Monday mornings to do a little breaking and entering. At least I hoped it would be little. I was afraid my breaking and entering skills would be a bit rusty (as in, never used before).

Despite my concerns, I nearly laughed out loud when I saw what Steph was wearing.

"Really?" I said, as I gave her a once over. She normally dressed in dark colors, but this head-to-toe black ensemble, topped by an unseasonably hot leather jacket, was maybe a bit over the top. Maybe.

Steph shrugged. "You said breaking and entering, I heard cat burglar." She returned my once-over gaze. "Not sure you're doing any better here."

I had gone for a business casual look that might blend into the background here in the downtown neighborhood where we had booked Lark's rental. I looked around at the sea of commuters streaming past us, then down at my oversized button-down and neatly cuffed ankle pants, topped off with a pair of loafers, all of which bore only a light spray of various paints and the crust of years-old clay splatter.

"Okay, yeah. Maybe we both have some work to do in the costume department," I grinned. "But whatever, we're here now. The apartment isn't far," I said and started to lead us the few blocks over to the apartment building. We were quiet as we walked, and I was thankful not to be met by the same barrage of questions that had been running through my mind all morning: *What if we can't get in? What if someone finds us there? Will the police somehow know we've been there?*

Luckily, the first part of getting in was easy: we always kept a spare key to the rental at school, in case any of the visiting artists got locked out. (Some other time I'll tell you about the drunken escapades that necessitated this policy.) Steph gave a quick, not at all subtle, glance over her shoulder as I unlocked the door to the apartment building and we slipped in.

On the second floor, we stood listening for a few minutes to make sure no one was about to come or go, although the only thing I could hear was the sound of my blood rushing in my ears. I slipped a canvas roll out of my purse, unrolling it to reveal a set of pottery tools. Only now did Steph's eyebrow raise.

"What's the plan here, Nancy Drew?" she asked. "Carve the door open? Sculpt the lock off?"

I glared at her, holding up a needle tool in reply. The thin metal needle was set into a smooth wooden handle, usually used for piercing or scoring pottery, and the perfect size and shape for a lock pick. I hoped.

"Okay, so you have a pottery lock pick." Steph raised her hands in defeat. "Let's see how it goes."

I slid the needle tool into the lock, wiggling it in what I hoped was a good approximation of every lock-picking scene in every movie I had ever seen. Taking a second, wider needle tool out of my roll, I slid it into the lock and turned it slightly to the left, keeping this pressure on the lock while I continued to wiggle at the pins with the first tool. Obviously, I had at least taken the time to watch a couple of lock-picking videos before coming down here this morning.

After a few minutes during which I learned that I could hold my breath for an extraordinary amount of time, the lock gave a final click and the door opened. I gave Steph a triumphant look before she pushed me into the apartment.

The apartment rental was a generous one bedroom with views of Boston Harbor (if you leaned yourself nearly halfway out the window). I looked around, doing a quick circuit of the space, before sharing a confused look with Steph.

"It doesn't look like anyone was staying here," she said, opening the fridge to reveal only a few bottles of water and a single grapefruit.

"There's only one small suitcase in the bedroom." I hauled out the bag in question, dumping it unceremoniously on the couch. Steph stood over my shoulder as we took in the contents.

"How long was his trip again?" Steph asked. "Because this looks like he packed for a long weekend. If that."

"Twelve days," I said, shaking my head as I considered how this man thought that two or three white button downs and a single pair of pants was adequate clothing for a trip that long. "It's as if Lark was so absorbed in his work, he couldn't be bothered with mundane things, like clean shirts."

A quick rummage to the bottom of the suitcase confirmed that there was no planner or notebook or even a single scrap of paper with a cryptic name on it, like Zeus or Night. Not that that would've been my first choice for a clue, but at least it would've been something.

"I'll take the rest of the kitchen and bathroom, you take the bedroom," Steph said, and I nodded my agreement, zipping up and returning the suitcase to where it had stood at the foot of the bed.

The bedroom was a bright, all white space that somehow seemed cozy instead of clinical. The harbor was the most visible from this window and I could picture waking up in the bed in its pile of blankets and happily getting a glimpse of sparkling water. Sure, I might have broken into a dead man's rented apartment and there was probably a ticking clock counting down to the time when we'd be caught here, but a girl could still have house envy.

I opened each drawer of the dresser, sweeping my hands to the back in the hope that Lark had stashed some secret message or dire warning in this otherwise unused dresser. I could hear Steph in the next room, the kitchen cabinets methodically opening and banging shut. I knelt to check the bottom drawer, and a small stack of books next to the bed caught my eye. I crawled over hurriedly (harder to do than it sounds) and grabbed the third book in the stack: a slim red volume that stood out in the stack of thick, glossy art books.

"Steph!" I called out. She hurried in, shushing me for shouting, which I ignored. "Look at this," I said, gesturing for her to join me on the floor and offering up the red notebook. We flipped through the pages together for a few minutes in silence.

"Does any of this mean anything to you?" Steph asked. "Honestly, to me it looks like a dream diary more than anything. It makes about as much sense as one."

"Mm, I don't think it's a dream journal," I said as I studied a page covered with what looked like notes for a sculpture. I pointed to a thick rectangle drawn around a mess of intersecting lines. "It's a sketchbook, of sorts. Plus, it looks like Lark made notes about his work in general." I pointed to the next page, where a series of phone numbers ran across the unlined page, each marked by a set of initials.

I read off one of the numbers and its initials. "BG ..." I said slowly, "I bet this is Betsy Gilbert. Rebecca's boss," I added at

Steph's blank look. "She owns a gallery downtown. I'd bet anything this is a list of galleries that Lark's been reaching out to, trying to get away from Giulia." I already had my phone out and was googling the number marked BG. I held up the screen triumphantly as the search pulled up Betsy Gilbert's gallery. I googled the next number listed and found a gallery with a Chelsea, New York address.

"Well, if there was any doubt about Lark trying to leave Giulia, I think we can put that to rest now," I said.

"True," Steph agreed, "But we haven't found anything about Monday night. These are just phone numbers. There's no dates or appointment times."

It felt like every time during this whole mess when I thought we had uncovered some groundbreaking new fact, it was quickly made useless. I was about to say as much when a couple of voices in the hallway silenced me. Steph clutched my arm and we both held our breath this time as we listened to the neighbors noisily descend the stairs.

"We should get out of here," she said as soon as the coast sounded clear. I slipped the notebook into my purse and we made a quick tour of the apartment, double checking that absolutely everything was exactly how we'd found it. I got a bit of side eye from Steph for pocketing the notebook, but what did she expect? I'd assumed the police had already gone through Lark's things here. If they didn't want a measly sketchbook, why shouldn't I have it? I stopped myself from wondering what a dead artist's sketchbook might be worth, and hurried to follow Steph out the door.

Over dinner with Arun that night, I decided to skip any summary of our activities that morning. He seemed so content, relaxed at our dining room table, as we tucked into large containers of noodles Arun had brought over from his mom. Why upset things? I already knew exactly what would happen if I came right out and told Arun that I had broken into a dead man's apartment that morning (did it help my defense that the apartment was just a vacation rental?), and that I had taken his sister with me, no less. His face would slowly cloud over, exactly like a big summer thunderstorm rolling in. See? If I knew what would happen clearly enough, I could consider myself punished already. Or that's what I told myself.

I had spent the afternoon going through Lark's notebook, which I briefly told Arun I had found in the faculty office suite. I almost hated to admit it, but the guy had some good ideas. I could only imagine what would happen if the notebook made its way into the hands of certain students in our department, particularly the guys who could reliably be found in the metalworking studios, welding whatever scraps together into something resembling a miniature Richard Serra. (Which was about the only kind of miniature I didn't like.)

"There were no appointments in the notebook," I was saying, having already told Arun about the list of phone numbers we had found. "Whatever Lark was doing on Monday night, he hadn't planned on it."

"So either he agreed in the moment to go upstairs with someone," Arun mused, "Or he was caught in the classroom unaware."

"But I can't think of anything Lark would have been doing in the classroom alone," I countered. I had already gone through these possibilities in the afternoon, and quickly discounted the idea that Lark had returned to a random sculpture classroom after his artist talk and … did something that I couldn't for the life of me think of, which probably meant this was the least likely scenario.

"Agreed," Arun said, "So I think we can assume that Lark went back upstairs with someone he already knew, whether he was planning on it or not." Arun paused, adorably in the middle of a bite of noodle. "So it would probably have to be someone that he felt comfortable enough with to make spur of the moment plans with. And to accept food or a drink from, since we know that he was poisoned." I agreed, since it was obvious that Lark wasn't nearly nice or gracious enough to be flexible around making sudden plans with other people.

"What about you?" I asked. "Did you have any more luck today than I did?"

Arun made a noncommittal head movement, somewhere between a nod and a shrug. "I looked through all the usual sources," he said, "general newspapers, art magazines, the university archives where he taught." Arun paused to take another bite. His nonchalance here already told me what he had found.

"And there wasn't anything too out of the ordinary," Arun said, confirming my suspicions. For all the man's horrid behavior, Lark did seem to have a talent for avoiding bad press, his behavior more of an open secret than front page news. "It was just the mix of exhibit reviews, tenure announcements, committee meeting minutes, and so on, that you'd expect for an artist who taught at the same university for as long as Lark did," Arun continued. "No reviews that were too horrible, no reports of Lark getting into some kind of fight or dispute. Nothing that would qualify as juicy gossip, or even mildly relevant news for us."

I nodded, trying not to make it seem like I was too disappointed at our lack of progress today.

"But then I checked our legal database …" Arun paused to drain the rest of his beer.

I almost kicked him, wishing I had spurs that could make him rush on.

"And I found that Lark was named in a lawsuit a few years ago," Arun finally continued, taking out his phone and tapping it open, then slid it over to me. "There were a couple of articles about it in the student newspaper," he said, nodding to the article that I was now reading on his phone screen. I continued to read the short blurb while Arun filled in the details. "From the lawsuit brief, it looks like there was an accident during the installation of Lark's work for a show at a museum in Chicago, about eight years ago. Apparently, one of the museum staff was injured badly enough to sue."

The article I was skimming confirmed what Arun said, with more details about the worker who was injured.

"It says here that the staff, this Robert Kelley guy, broke his leg and foot in multiple places." I looked up. "What the hell happened?" I hoped that Arun would say that Kelley got a six-figure settlement. Instead, Arun simply shook his head.

"They settled out of court, so I don't know the final details," he said. "From the other articles I saw, it sounds like a piece of Lark's fell during the install, landing on this poor guy. The museum and Lark were both named in the lawsuit, so I'm assuming that the fall was probably precipitated by something specific Lark did or didn't do. Since they settled, I'd guess that the museum's insurance paid it out."

"Did you find out anything else about Robert Kelley?" I asked, scrolling through the rest of the article to see if there was a photo of him anywhere. I was oddly hopeful that by some freak coincidence, he happened to live in Boston now and was prone to fits of vengeful rage.

"I searched around about him a bit more, but obviously Robert and Kelley are not uncommon names," Arun replied. "But if it's the same person, then it looks like Robert Kelley now works at a university gallery in Providence. I found him on the staff page on their website."

"So he lives about an hour away. Maybe a bit longer at rush hour," I mused aloud, thinking of the time of day that Lark was killed. Arun gave me a warning look that I knew all too well.

"Just because this guy lives *somewhat* close by," Arun started, with a heavy emphasis on somewhat, "doesn't mean that he killed Lark. Robert Kelley would had to have known that Lark was in Boston, at the school that night, and he would've had to get Lark to go upstairs with him." Arun paused, the warning look still in place, cutting off whatever weak retort I could have given.

"That said," Arun continued, "I was thinking that, as a journalist writing a story about Lark, it would only be reasonable and responsible for me to call Robert tomorrow. To gather background."

My face lit up, even if Arun was still holding up a hand to indicate that I needed to slow my roll. Not that that gesture usually worked on me.

"And as a responsible journalist, you should definitely have an assistant there when you call him," I added, hoping Arun would be dazzled enough by my bright smile to agree before he could start to question his journalistic ethics. "I can take notes for you!"

Arun bit back a grin. "I suppose that some journalists may have an assistant," he replied. "Who would sit quietly and listen in, only to take notes." I ignored the limitations he was emphasizing and slid over one chair, leaning in to hug him. We sat quietly for a second, enjoying the miraculously empty apartment I had at the moment, where we could actually hug for a minute without Rebecca clucking in the background or Mel making salacious faces at us.

Arun's phone was still on the table in front of us, and I glanced down at the article again, noticing the title of the exhibit in the headline. I picked up the phone, searching for the exhibit that they had been installing at the time of the accident. Arun looked over my shoulder as I opened the exhibit catalog, still posted on the museum's website. I groaned as my eyes skimmed down the list of participating artists on the front page of the catalog.

"What?" Arun asked, then added an "oh" as he caught up, reading the same name in the list of artists that I had seen: James Thompson. "Well," Arun said, squeezing me on the arm like he was pumping up an athlete about to go up to bat, "just think of it this way: If you talk to Thompson in the morning, and he hopefully remembers all about the accident during the exhibit, then you get to fill in the details later when I graciously allow you to sit in on my interview with Robert Kelley."

I pondered what would really make having to talk to James Thompson worth it. Unbidden, an image of Agnes came to mind and I kicked myself for my petty reluctance.

"You're right," I said and nodded, straightening up as if ready to face battle. "Knowing Thompson, he probably remembers every minute of the accident and will relish the chance to tell me all about it." Or at least, I very much hoped that's what was about to happen. I had decided to try and catch Thompson early in the morning the next day, before classes started. Hopefully he wouldn't already be surrounded by his usual circle of devotees, a group of students who endlessly milled around him, apparently just taking in his glory via osmosis. I had had only a few run-ins with Thompson before, mostly while I was trying to figure out what had happened to my friend, Catherine. She worked closely with him at the time, and I could never understand what this otherwise intelligent, sweet person saw in him. To me, Professor James Thompson acted like a mascot for every smarmy, ultimately insecure but never able to admit it, artist, who thrived in a position of power where he could feel more secure. A lot like Lark, come to think of it.

Of course, for now, I had to plaster on my most ingratiating grin and join the masses who revered him. I had even tried to comb my hair for the occasion, choosing to wear a light blue chambray button-down that I hoped screamed "casual but professional artist whom you can absolutely spill your guts to." Although I wasn't sure what my ripped jeans screamed.

I walked into the faculty offices with about twenty minutes before I had to get to class, my heart sinking at the silence coming from the series of cubicles in the room. Certain that everyone was already out, setting up for class in their respective classrooms, I jumped about a mile at the loud scrape of a chair being pushed back.

Thompson stood against the door to his cubicle, at the back of the room. "Samantha," he called out, always pretending to forget that I went by Sam, as if anyone were too busy to remember a three-letter word. "What can I do for you this fine morning?"

I plastered on the grin I most definitely had to practice in the mirror earlier, and made my way back to his office in what I hoped looked like a casual saunter, something that said I was confident but also needed help. What he actually thought about me at this moment was anyone's guess, his grin perpetually inscrutable.

"There is actually something you can help me with," I said, taking the seat he gestured to next to his desk. I had printed out the front cover of the exhibit catalog earlier that morning, and took it out of my bag now, smoothing out the paper onto his desk.

Thompson picked up the paper and gave a slow whistle as he took in the graphics on the cover and the names of artists listed neatly in the corner. "This brings back some memories," he said. "Not sure what it has to do with you, though." My smile faltered a bit at that. You could never quite tell with Thompson when he was genuinely challenging you and when he was just pulling your leg – anything to make an otherwise simple conversation that bit more difficult. I had never had much patience for people like that and I took a deep breath now, reminding myself that I was really here for Agnes.

"I know about the accident that happened during the install of this show," I started, then tried not to trip over myself too badly as I backpedaled. "Well, I know that an accident happened and that an art handler named Robert Kelley was injured. But I'm sure that there are a lot of details I don't know. Details that you could probably fill in."

Thompson nodded, continuing to study the page in front of him. "Are you doing this because of Agnes?" he asked without looking up. Thankfully, that meant he didn't see the look of utter shock that passed over my face.

"Um, yes," I stammered. "I mean, yeah. How do you know that?" I hadn't really told anyone outside of my immediate friends about all of this, and so far our activities had been limited to run of the mill things like following broke gallerists and breaking into dead people's apartments. I hadn't been asking a ton of obvious questions all over campus, nothing that should have caught the attention of someone like Thompson.

"You obviously care about her a lot, and everyone knows about how the police have been interviewing her pretty much every day," Thompson said, as if in answer to my silent questions. He finally looked up as he continued, "Agnes is a good person. She doesn't deserve to be treated like this. She's lucky to have you on her side." Thompson nodded as if in agreement with himself.

I stammered a quick thank you, taken aback at the genuine sentiments he was apparently able to communicate. Maybe the trick was to catch him early in the morning, before Thompson was fully awake and the gate of smarminess had come down.

"So, do you actually remember this?" I asked, nodding toward the printout. "What happened with the accident?"

Thompson nodded. "I was in town for the install, working with the crew at the museum to install one of my pieces in the show. This big thing full of styrofoam peanuts." He waved his hands as if this was a full explanation of the artwork, or as if to dismiss some younger folly. "I wasn't there on the actual day that it happened," Thompson continued. "But it was all that anyone was talking about for days afterward. Apparently, they were handling some big piece of Lark's, and the sculpture fell on one of the art handlers. Bob, I think his name was."

"Robert Kelley," I said, filling in the blank.

"Right, Robert. I think he was pretty badly injured. I didn't see him again after the accident," he said.

"And what about Lark?" I asked.

"What about Lark?" Thompson replied. "He didn't want to

have anything to do with it. Afterwards, Lark would tell anyone who listened that it was the fault of the art handlers, that other crews had installed that same piece with no issues before. I don't know what happened in court, but I think Robert sued Lark."

"And the museum," I added. I wasn't at all surprised to hear that Lark never even came close to admitting culpability in the accident. I couldn't understand how you could know that someone had broken a limb because of your artwork, and never even have the urge to apologize.

Thompson shrugged. "And I'm sorry to say, that's pretty much all I know. Some poor kid was practically crushed to death under one of Lark's monstrosities, and Lark never did anything even remotely close to apologizing," he summarized. Thompson must have seen the look on my face. "What?" he continued. "Did you think that just because we're men who make sculptures and move in more or less the same circles, I'd automatically love Lark? I'm just as capable as anyone of recognizing him for the bombastic, cruel man that he was." Thompson rose, as if propelled by the force of his feelings about Lark. "And now, if you'll excuse me, I have to get to class." He gathered a stack of books sitting on the desk and paused in the entrance to his office. "Whenever you're ready to leave Martina and switch to me as your faculty advisor, let me know," Thompson added, calling out a goodbye over his shoulder.

I sat there for a few moments, still clutching the paper with the exhibit details on it. I shook my head to clear it, brushing off Thompson's last remarks. I wasn't sure what else this conversation gained us, except that I perhaps, strangely, had found someone else interested in helping Agnes. I bent to gather up my backpack, pausing mid-bend as another thought came to me. I had also found someone else who seemed to dislike Lark, maybe even more vehemently than anyone else I had talked to.

Chapter 16

I snuck into Martina's class a few minutes late, embarrassed to be late since I was technically there as the TA. It seemed crazy to think that just a week ago, I had found a dead body in this very classroom – a classroom that, judging from the looks on about half our students' faces, was most definitely feeling pretty haunted. Luckily for those who looked the most worried about the room they were standing in, today was the day that students would be trained on our metalworking and welding equipment. Hopefully the sparks would drive out any Lark-related ghosts or ill vibes. Plus, you couldn't be both worried about ghosts and operating a MIG welder at the same time.

Martina shuffled over to me while the metal studio technician went over basic safety procedures at the front of the room. I had made a little perch for myself in the back of the classroom where I could guzzle my coffee in relative peace and, even subliminally, get as much distance as I could from the spot where Lark had been found. The floor had been scrubbed clean (were there special janitors who came with the police or did our usual janitors do this?), but I thought I could still see the rusty remnants of all that fake blood.

"How've you been doing, Sam?" Martina was whispering to

me. "With everything going on?"

I nodded in reply, as if yes meant good. "Okay," I managed, still not quite awake enough for long sentences and still too distracted by my conversation with Thompson to come up with anything more detailed than that.

"I'm getting more worried about Agnes." Martina leaned closer to me, dropping her voice even lower. "I saw her yesterday after class and she looked just completely exhausted. I hate to say it, but she was really looking her age. For the first time since I met her."

"Oh," I said, a little taken aback at her forthrightness. I wasn't even sure what Agnes's age was, exactly, and definitely not sure how to reply to Martina's comments in a way that wouldn't get me in trouble with HR. When is it ever a good idea to comment on how old someone looks?

Luckily, Martina hardly seemed to notice my lack of response. "I mean, she just seemed completely out of it yesterday," Martina continued. "Agnes was asking me these really crazy questions." Martina waited a beat as the studio technician turned on the welder, the sound momentarily drowning out her whisper. "I encouraged her to take some time off from work. I really think she needs to get some rest." I made a noncommittal head movement in reply, which apparently looked more committal than I realized.

"I think you should encourage her to take some time off, too," Martina said. "I know Agnes really values your opinion."

"I'll mention it to her," I replied, momentarily blindsided by the idea that Agnes might value my opinion even half as much as I valued hers. The truth was, as worried as I was about Agnes, obviously, I think the last thing she needed to do right now was leave school. I know Detective O'Connor could be reasonable, but I didn't think it was a good look to seem like she was running away from the investigation. I chalked up Martina's fears to the fact that she just hadn't known Agnes as long. I was about to say as much to her when we were interrupted by a student coming over to ask about getting appropriate footwear.

I hopped off my perch on the desk, biting my tongue to keep from making a snide remark as I glanced down and saw the socks-and-sandals combo he had chosen to wear even though he knew today was a metal working day. I launched into a standard lecture on closed toe shoes, gesturing toward my own worn, faded blue hiking boots. I rolled my eyes toward Martina as the student sloped off to rejoin the group, but she still looked about a million miles away, her brow knitted behind her heavy black glasses. Not wanting to press the topic any further, I settled in silently next to her, and we watched as a series of sparks lit up the studio.

After a morning spent standing in the back of the classroom, trying to avoid sparks as the students fumbled their way through welding, I couldn't run out of the department building fast enough. Arun had texted me near the end of class, confirming that I could meet him at our usual coffeeshop over lunch while he called Robert Kelley.

I walked into the cafe, only my usual ten minutes late, and slid into the chair across from Arun after giving him a quick kiss hello. I was eager to get the call started, and not only because I had to get back to work in the library after our lunch break, but Arun insisted on reviewing the terms we had agreed to last night. I nodded as I agreed once again that I wouldn't interject too much, I wouldn't ask leading questions (too much, I added silently), and I would generally avoid compromising Arun's journalistic integrity. Given that I wasn't exactly going to write an article about the guy, I didn't see how this last piece was really possible, but I didn't argue.

I could feel my heart speeding up as Arun finally started to dial Robert Kelley's number, sliding the phone onto the table between us, the recording function already on. After the fifth ring, I was about to open my mouth to ask what our plan B was if he didn't answer, when suddenly there was a click on the line.

"Hello?" Robert answered.

"Hi, is this Robert Kelley?" Arun replied in a voice that I hadn't heard before, somehow deeper and more professional than his regular voice. I had to admit, it was oddly reassuring. At least one of us sounded confident.

"Speaking. Can I ask who's calling?"

"My name is Arun Phan. I'm a journalist," Arun said, mentioning the name of his newspaper. "I'm working on a story about the recent death of the artist Lark Harrier and I was hoping you could answer a few questions for me. I'm also here with Samantha Green, my assistant."

There was silence on the line as Robert seemed to be making his mind up. I kicked Arun (gently) under the table, urging him to say something else to get Robert onboard.

"I'm just looking to fill in some background information, get a little more detail on what Lark was like as a person, or to work with," Arun said. "You wouldn't have to be named in the article at all."

Robert cleared his throat and sighed, seemingly prolonging his decision. "Yeah," he said eventually, "I wondered how long it would be before someone called me about this. If it's just background info and I'm not named, I'm happy to answer some questions."

"That's great, I really appreciate it," Arun said as I beamed triumphantly at him. "To start with, could you tell me a bit about how you knew Lark?"

"Well, I'm going to assume you already know about the accident, or you wouldn't be calling me," Robert replied, letting our silence speak for itself. "I met Lark for the first time during the installation of a group exhibit at the Chicago Modern Museum, where I used to work."

"And what was it like working with Lark?" Arun asked. "Even before the accident."

There was a pause, and I could sense Robert deciding what tone to strike. Since we all already knew what kind of person Lark could be, I didn't want to risk losing information if Robert felt like he couldn't be straight (i.e., brutally honest) with us.

"This is Sam," I cut in, "I actually had a chance to meet Lark before he died. I have a feeling we probably had similar experiences of working with him."

Robert gave a low chuckle. "I'm sure we probably did. Honestly, working with Lark wasn't even the worst thing during the installation, not at first. He was demanding, and he was picky about how we placed his sculpture, but not much worse than any of the other artists."

"What else was going on?" Arun asked. "You said it wasn't the worst thing. What was making the install so difficult?"

"The whole thing that happened with Lark's work was just the last straw in an already tense situation," Robert said. "The other staff at the museum never really understood what our job was as art handlers, so they were always asking us to do things that were impossible to do safely in the time we had.

Like, this one time a curator wanted us to move a series of massive paintings on a day when we only had two guys on the crew. It was always like that, the staff wanting us to do things that would've wound up hurting one of us or the art itself."

"Which it did, eventually," I said. "Is that what happened with Lark's work?"

"We never had the budget for exactly the right materials, so everything was always a little slapdash, a little haphazard," Robert said. I was struggling to maintain an open mind as he detailed the hazardous conditions that had led to his breaking a leg. I know we were looking for the actual murderer, someone who could free Agnes from her current situation, but I hoped we didn't have the right person. Not this time.

"When we went to install Lark's piece," Robert was saying, "we couldn't get the proper rigging equipment we needed to lift the piece into place. Lark insisted that other crews had installed it without the tools I was asking for, so the curator wouldn't approve the budget. So we made do and constructed a rigging system for one of those huge steel and plexi pieces of … things Lark does." Robert gave another low chuckle. "We were installing outside, in the rain no less, because we were running behind on the install and Lark's piece couldn't wait another day. But then the whole thing just fell apart. The strapping slipped and the piece came right down on me."

Even knowing what was coming, I couldn't hide my sharp gasp. From the sympathetic look on Arun's face, he was feeling the same way.

"You know, my lawyer thought it was a surefire win," Robert continued. His voice had the far-off quality of someone recalling a memory they had retold countless times already. "We had a whole laundry list of safety issues that anyone on the staff would have confirmed. But no one was actually willing to come forward and testify. There was no union, nothing to protect anyone. So the best my lawyer could do was settle out of court, taking a payout from the museum's insurance that was only half what we were asking for."

"That must have been infuriating," Arun said. "Did you ever try to do anything else, after the lawsuit? To talk to Lark about it or anything?"

"I mean, my leg and foot were broken in multiple places, so I couldn't exactly go racing after Lark. And even if I could have, what was I going to do? Beg him to apologize?"

Robert Kelley might not have been able to run after Lark immediately after the accident, but that didn't mean he couldn't run now.

"Can I ask another question?" I didn't wait for a reply. "Sorry if this seems really random, but could you tell us where you were last Monday evening?"

There was a pause long enough for me to worry that I had overstepped my bounds. I looked down at the phone, willing Robert to answer while I pointedly avoided Arun's look.

"Since you say you're journalists, and not cops, I'm going to assume you have a random reason for asking that, and you're not asking because you're somehow investigating Lark's death," Robert finally replied. "I was out of the country all of last week. I work at a university museum here in Providence now, and I've been on a courier trip to the UK since the Friday before last. I only got back home on Saturday."

I bit back panic as I realized we had no real way of confirming what was otherwise a pretty rock-solid alibi. I felt completely torn between wanting to save Agnes and not wanting Robert Kelley to be the real killer.

"I appreciate you answering that," Arun said with one final glare at me.

I gave a small shrug, since he really should have known that I was going to have to say something like that. Otherwise, what was the point of this call?

"It's fine," Robert replied. "Honestly, even if I could, I wouldn't have done anything. Lark deserved to maybe lose some work, some money, anything that would've deflated his ego a bit. But no one deserves to die over something like this. At the end of the day, regardless of whose fault it was that created the situation, it really was just an accident."

I sat there, swimming in an odd mix of emotions, while Arun politely signed off the call. You had to admire the apparent grace with which Robert seemed to accept the accident. Would I be able to react with such a similar state of zen? I could picture Stephanie laughing in response to that question.

"Well, that was … interesting," Arun said after saving the recording and packing his phone and notepad back into his bag. "I can call around and see if there are any records about Robert's courier trip, but he's right. We're not cops. No one has to tell a journalist anything they don't want to."

"It's okay," I sighed. "This was, as they say, a very promising lead. But I just don't think he's our guy." I took a huge gulp of my coffee to hide the obvious disappointment on my face. "I tried not to get my hopes up too much …" I trailed off.

"I know it's tough, Sam," Arun said, leaning over the table to take my hand. "But it's worth it for us to look into everything, to be methodical."

I nodded, agreeing that we would meet up later and maybe go to the movies, do anything to get our minds off this. But methodical? My brain felt about as far from methodical as it could right now. I felt like I was swimming in a sea of suspects, each one at once likely and ludicrously unlikely. Right now, I think I'd believe it if you told me it was the cook in the library with the candlestick.

Chapter 17

I had hoped that the quiet of the bright, airy library would help me feel a little more balanced and calm. Unfortunately, it was an hour into my afternoon shift and so far, I had spent half of the time reshelving books and the other half frustrated about Lark. As far as I could see, Lark was a generally disliked, not particularly nice person, from whose death at least a few people would have definitely benefited, while others would have been able to exact revenge, perhaps a revenge they had even been pondering for years. My mind darkened as I knew that the police saw Agnes in this last category. I mentally crossed off her name, penciling in Robert Kelley's instead.

Yet, despite what seemed like my pick of suspects, there was no one who really seemed able to have committed Lark's murder in this very particular, dramatic way. There were too many people on my list of suspects who just wouldn't have been able to get into the building without anyone noticing and remembering. I think. And the people who were already in the building, like Professor Thompson, were not necessarily the strongest suspects. I sighed, remembering the time that Thompson had been my number one suspect in Catherine's death. I really had to stop blaming the guy for every murder that happened on campus. Or maybe he should stop acting like such a suspect.

I tried to think back through all the Agatha Christies I had read as a kid, devouring each book in a matter of days, usually while tucked under the covers with a flashlight. She did love her locked room mysteries, but I struggled to think of one that fit this particular scenario. I sighed, knowing it was a pointless thought exercise. I loved Christie as much as the next person, but I knew that the problem with comparing her plots to real life was that in real life, people just don't have that mysterious first wife or long-lost sibling that her crimes often relied on.

I was just about to commence yet another celebration of my personal pity party when Charles came strolling into the library. The burgeoning performance artist had an oversized backpack slung over his shoulder, the kind of thing you might use for a weekend-long camping trip. Or to carry a lot of material to and from school if you were planning on staging an artistic crime scene.

I briefly considered ways I could casually go up and question him, when he turned toward the circulation desk.

"I'm looking for a book that's required for class," he asked me. I hurried to put on my most composed librarian face while I continued to try and decide how best to ask him about his feelings on Lark, what he was doing sneaking into the sculpture studio where the material to make the crime scene evidence had clearly been stashed, and, oh, you know, did he kill our most recent visiting artist.

"So?" Charles was asking. "Do you know where I can find books on the history of video in performance art?"

"Of course, yes," I said, getting up and coming around the desk. "Right this way." It was perhaps overkill to personally walk him over to the shelf that was only twenty feet away and which I could easily have pointed to, but the rows of shelves provided cover and privacy. Key features for cornering someone in a private conversation.

"This is the section here," I said, gesturing to a row of books in the middle of the shelving that ran along the far back wall. Charles acknowledged this with a quick nod and a muttered thanks, and quickly got to work scanning the titles.

"Oh, by the way, is this for your work in the sculpture area?" I asked, knowing how stupid I sounded given that Charles had just said he needed books on video and performance art, but casual segues weren't really my strong suit. "I'm sorry I interrupted your work the other day, in the Trash Can."

I watched as Charles straightened up from looking at the shelf, slowly turning a shade of lobster red brighter than anything I had seen outside of an actual lobster. If this was his poker face, I knew whom I wanted to play against.

"It's fine, it's no problem," Charles said, "I don't really … I don't work in the sculpture studios too much. It's not really serious."

"Oh, but you must make all those plates yourself, right? The ones you were using at the show over the weekend? We were there," I added unnecessarily, as the other shoe had already dropped the minute I mentioned the dinner plates.

"Look, I know I did in the public performance, but it's not really something …" Charles trailed off and I waited silently for him to continue. "The whole smashing pottery thing is something my therapist suggested. It's really a private thing, and I don't even know why I did it on Saturday, it was just like a draft. Something I was trying out. Usually, I just use the Trash Can a couple times a week. It's not a big deal. Sorry if I freaked you out the other day."

"So, you don't actually work on anything in the Trash Can?" I asked. "I mean, you don't make new work. You just go in there to smash some pottery in a messy workplace." This last comment wasn't even a question, as I realized that I had been pretty far off the mark about Charles. Or at least about his presence in the sculpture area, which, it was true, was not a crime. In and of itself.

"Yeah, exactly," Charles said. "Again, sorry if I freaked you out or something the other day. Usually that room is empty."

"I know," I said slowly. Maybe even if this was a dead end, Charles could still be somewhat helpful. "Have you seen anyone else in there in the past week or so? Working with a big box of materials. Mostly fabrics?"

"Why?" he asked.

Fair enough.

"Oh, I had some supplies out and a few things went missing," I said, laughing at myself for my own pretend mistake. "I was just wondering if anyone had seen anything."

Charles shook his head. "I only use the room when it's empty." His eyes turned back to the books on the shelf and I worried that I had lost him. "Although actually, I did see a big box of fabric and stuff out the other day. Last week. On one of the tables, like someone had been working and left suddenly."

"Thanks," I replied, "that's really helpful. Although you don't know who it might have been?"

"Sorry, no," he said, shaking his head. "There were a couple teachers in the hallway as I walking in, and I stopped to say hello to Professor Thompson. But there was no one in the studio itself."

"Thanks, no worries. I'm sure my stuff will turn up soon," I said and turned to leave before he could ask me any questions about my supposed "stuff."

Back at the circulation desk, I studiously avoided the ever-increasing stack of books waiting to be reshelved, and settled into my chair to think. Hopefully this time without doing my whole pity party thing.

So, Professor Thompson could be placed at or near the scene where the faux crime scene evidence had been made. And he was a painting professor, I reasoned, who wouldn't have raised any eyebrows if he had been walking around the building carrying a gallon of red paint.

But there was something bothering me about this whole idea, and even the very fact that Lark had been killed here, at our school and in Boston. I know there are people around who had plenty of good reasons to kill Lark, but not many who also had ample access to the means of killing him. What if I had been looking in the wrong place this whole time? What if whoever killed Lark wasn't connected to him here in Boston, but was related to his life and his past in Chicago?

Not that I knew anyone other than Agnes who had known Lark before. It's true that Thompson had been in a group show with him at least once before, but I racked my brains now as I tried to recall whether Thompson ever said he actually met Lark during that show. I sighed, realizing that technically, Thompson had only talked about Lark's behavior after the accident, which Thompson wasn't even there for, and which I guess he could have just as easily heard about from others as witnessed himself.

I was interrupted as two girls walked into the library, coming over to the circulation desk. One of the girls, a freshman I vaguely knew as being friends with one of the students in

Martina's class, slid a book across the desk to me.

"Just returning this!" she chirped, with a wave of her hand, complete with sparkly purple-painted nails.

I picked up the proffered book, studying the cover and its layers of black-and-white images: *Collage and Assemblage: A brief history*. Perhaps the bubbly girl had the right idea. Maybe what I needed to do was collage Thompson onto Lark's past (or whatever other messy artistic metaphor made more sense). In any event, I could comb back through the articles and materials Arun had found about Lark, and look for anywhere that Thompson was mentioned or was likely to have been around for. Was there any way I could cross-reference their exhibition history, to see how many shows they had been in together? At least the cross-referencing would make my boss at the library proud. Or maybe Thompson had been passed over for a job or an exhibit, in favor of Lark. Who knew how small an incident could provoke such an act? With this cheery thought, I put my head down and got back to work.

Unfortunately, I had then spent the evening having a somewhat demoralizing dinner with Rebecca, who was not as taken with my whole "James Thompson must have killed somebody, why not Lark" line of thinking. Instead, she had gone on and on about keeping an open mind, giving someone the benefit of the doubt, and about every other variation on that sentiment that you can imagine.

As such, I woke up the next morning all the more determined to prove – fairly – that it was Thompson after all. I had a suspicion (or at least a hope) that there were a few people on campus I hadn't talked to yet who might be able to fill in some missing info. I would just have to fit these interviews into an otherwise busy day of class and work in the library.

Heading back into school with renewed purpose, I didn't even stop out front for my usual pre-class cigarette, instead heading straight into the studio for Agnes's class. As I walked down the hall toward the room where "Alternative Materials" met, I watched as Martina and Agnes stepped out of the classroom, lingering in the hall to talk. I paused, about to wave to them both, when something about their vibe stopped me in my tracks.

Martina had her back to me, but I could see the tension in the set of her shoulders and the way she was clutching a bright blue thermos in one hand, the white knuckles on a book in her other hand. Not wanting to intrude, I ducked back around the corner of the hall, peering out to study the thoughtful look on Agnes's face. Although her mouth was set in a downward turn, her eyebrows drawn together, her eyes still held their characteristic warmth. So, she was concerned but not angry. Martina was shaking her head. She gave a small shrug and turned to go.

I whipped my head back around the corner, then proceeded to walk down the hallway casually as if I hadn't just seen this exchange. I gave Martina a broad smile and a wave, receiving only a curt nod in return.

Agnes was still standing in the doorway to the studio and I shot her a questioning look as I walked up. She smiled thoughtfully at me, the smile not quite dissolving the furrow in her brow.

"Good morning, Samantha," she greeted me. "Care to help me set up for today? I'd like the desks back in rows for these presentations." Agnes always assigned students different topics from the course syllabus, tasking us with teaching one another.

I silently got to work rearranging the desks into neat rows, considering how best to ask about whatever she and Martina had been discussing.

"I hope you're doing okay this week. I know this whole thing has been so tough on you. And I'm sure on Martina, too," I tried.

Agnes smiled, murmuring noncommittally as she shuffled a stack of papers at a table near the front of the room. Apparently the "in" I had as a TA, whatever access I had been granted to peek behind the curtains of the faculty wizardry, only extended so far. I opened my mouth to try another approach but was cut short by the arrival of three other students, annoyingly on time today. If Agnes wasn't going to tell me what was going on while we were alone, she definitely wasn't going to tell me with other kids in the room.

I settled into a chair in the back, biding my time as the first student got up to present on the intersection of text and sculpture, cycling through images of the iconic LOVE sculptures alongside more contemporary pieces that utilized empty billboards. Interesting as it might have been, I snuck out of the darkened classroom about halfway through, heading back down to the lobby.

Our security guards might have been something of a running joke to the student body, routinely the subject of punchlines as they continued to "persecute" (to whatever extent they really could) minor "crimes" like having forgotten the necessary ID to get into the building, while they looked the other way as kids smoked pot in the secluded darkroom. Still, they had eyes and they were stationed at the front door of our building. So, I figured, if anyone had seen someone out of place coming or going the night Lark was killed, there was a good chance it was one of these guys. Sure, they might have already told the police. But the police might not have known about everyone to ask about.

I had printed out a series of small photos the night before, ranging from a professional headshot of Cam, our local workspace manager, to a blurry image of Robert Kelly taken from his sparsely populated social media presence. I clutched the folder of photos now as I walked up to the security desk, beaming – half because I wanted to seem like a harmless student with a silly project and half out of relief to see that it was the usual guard who worked Mondays and Wednesdays.

"Good morning!" I trilled, walking up and placing the folder on the desk. "Would you happen to have a moment to help me? It shouldn't take more than a few minutes."

The guard, a heavyset man with "Diego" on a small gold name badge over his breast pocket, smiled indulgently down at me. I had never exchanged more than a passing hello with him before, but knew he'd been here long enough to develop the same attitude as a lot of the staff: an ever-so-slightly condescending acceptance of art students and their capricious whims. He nodded, gesturing for me to continue. I opened the folder and spread the photos out across Diego's desk, lining them right side up toward him. I pointed to the first one, an image of Giulia cropped out of a photo taken at one of her gallery openings.

"Is there any chance you saw this woman, or any of the other people in these photos, last Monday? Anyone who was coming into or out of the building in the late afternoon, early evening?" I paused as he studied each image in turn, biting my lip to keep from hurrying him along with more questions.

Diego shook his head slowly. "There was a lot going on

last Monday," he said eventually. "A lot of people coming and going."

I nodded, aiming for a look of commiseration. "I know, and I'm sorry for asking, but it's really important. Could you please take a second look? Any of these people would have been leaving school last Monday evening, sometime after six or seven pm." A slight look of impatience passed over Diego's face, but he still pointedly looked down at the photos again. I guess the whims of art students were still trying, no matter how long you'd worked around them. I tried to keep my face polite and casual, like this was a regular thing, not a murder thing.

"Look, I'm sorry I can't help you better. But I really haven't seen any of these people on campus. Last Monday or anytime." Diego sat back down in finality, picking up his walkie talkie and fiddling with the controls. Taking the hint, I shuffled the photos back into the folder, stumbling over myself to thank him effusively.

"Of course, of course. I really appreciate the help," I said as I backed away, turning down the nearest hallway and pausing as soon as I was out of sight. I opened the folder again now that I was alone, and looked down on the images of Cam, Giulia, and Robert, with a few random people sprinkled in (a trick I had probably learned, or imagined learning, from television).

I snapped the folder shut again, more resolved than ever. I know it was only one person's word, but it seemed definitive enough for me: Whoever killed Lark was someone already in the building, whose presence that night would have been unremarkable. Someone like a professor.

After that morning's revelations, the rest of the day passed by uneventfully, for better or worse. The library had quickly filled up that afternoon as midterms were already approaching. I knew from experience that this week (with about two weeks to go), we'd get the first wave of students who would prepare early and seriously; next week, the second wave who would do a good show of studying but put in only a few hours; and the final week, when the rest of the student body came in, who would have to pull all-nighters to get all their studying in on time. I say this with no shade – I was in the last group, for sure.

As busy as it was, I still managed to duck out a few minutes early. There was one last conversation I was hoping to have that day. I slipped out of the library, heading over to our school's gallery one floor below.

"Bridget, hi!" I called to the woman who was gathering her things in the gallery's small office. "Glad I caught you here!"

Poor Bridget froze like a deer in headlights. True, she probably had no idea who I was, let alone why I'd be happy to catch her. She stammered a hello.

"Wild week we've been having, isn't it?" I said, coming into the office and dropping my bag on the desk nonchalantly, like it was a totally routine occurrence for me to ambush the gallery assistant while she tried to leave work for the day. "It seems like about forever ago that we were setting up for that awful artist's talk."

The gears clicked into place and I saw Bridget realize where she had met me. "Oh, right, you're the girl with the projector," she blurted out. I tried not to blush.

"Yep, that's me, projector girl," I said with what I hoped was a confident grin and not an absolute grimace at the memory of how all this started. Remembering the way Bridget had been practically cowering in the corner that day, I put on an exaggerated expression of sympathy. "It must have been a really tough day for you, too," I said. "I know working with Lark couldn't have been easy."

"Yeah, well, I mostly just tried to stay out of the way," Bridget replied, seemingly more comfortable now that she remembered who I was. She continued scooping books and papers off the desk and tucking them into her neat black carryall. I rushed on, anxious to stall her as long as I needed to.

"Did something happen earlier in the day?" I asked with a knowing look.

"No, it wasn't like that," she said. "I stayed out of the way as best I could from the start." She paused, looking at me as she clearly considered how much to let spill. "You know, I heard that Lark had gotten multiple staff fired from his university's gallery. For doing a 'bad job' on some show of his," she said, rolling her eyes.

I widened my own in response. "Wow, that's ridiculous. Not exactly surprising, though. You don't happen to know who it was that he had fired, do you?"

Bridget shook her head. "Honestly, I'm sure there's a long list of people he had fired or blacklisted for one petty reason or another. But I don't know who these specific people were. I just know what I heard." She grabbed a red jacket from a coat hook in the corner and heaved her bag up. "Now, if you'll excuse me, I really have to get home."

"Of course, absolutely. Nice to chat," I said, stepping out of the way so she could squeeze past me, out the door of the small office. I stood where I was even after Bridget had left. Like the gallery assistant, I was also sure there was a long list of people Lark had gotten fired or blacklisted. The only thing was, would I be able to find everyone on it? And, even more importantly, would a certain professor be included? I tapped on my phone, clicking open my calendar and seeing a beautiful, shining free period on it for tomorrow afternoon: the perfect time to do a little archival sleuthing. Who knew how many years of school records I would have to comb through to find any reference to Thompson? But I would do it, because the university Lark worked for was just prestigious enough that I could see, maybe, killing someone over it. I mean, it wasn't like an Ivy League-level reason for murder, and was I grasping at straws? Hopefully not.

Chapter 18

I groaned inwardly as I watched the golden light filtering through the library windows, picking out dust motes in the otherwise pristine space and signaling the impending end of the day. I spent the next afternoon in the library of the business school, located in the building directly across the street from the art department, positioned as if to highlight our two discordant professions. I had hoped the change in scenery would jog some creative thinking, or at the very least good luck, but I had so far spent several hours combing through school records, faculty meeting minutes, and student newspaper articles, and only found myself hopping from one rabbit hole to the next, with no mention of James Thompson in sight.

In the past decade of Lark's career, three people had been turned down for tenure at his university, a number that seemed oddly high when I considered the otherwise low turnover in our own department. I soon found myself searching for each of them in turn, trying to find any clues as to their current whereabouts. As if a bland social media profile could really tell me whether someone would be willing to get coldblooded revenge for a decade-old slight.

The first two people had similar careers since their failure to secure tenure under Lark's watch. Both had continued to show at mid-size galleries around the country, and both now worked for liberal arts colleges. One was on the East Coast (although three hours away in Connecticut, and yes, I did check the rush-hour driving times), and one was on the West Coast. Now, I was deep in the rabbit hole of looking for the lone woman on my list, an Isabella Gray. Other than her great aptronym, I was having a hard time finding anything else out about her. There were a couple of enraged student articles in the school newspaper after she was passed over, but it didn't look like they had changed much about the situation, and she resigned not long after. After that, there were a couple small mentions of Gray on the websites of local community galleries she had shown with, but it seemed as if she had otherwise dropped off the face of the earth. Or at least off the face of the art world.

I clicked on one more gallery link, buried deep on the tenth page of search results in a sea of random people's phone numbers. I promised myself this was the last link I'd follow. After all, what did I expect? Was I really going to find anything different if I kept at it till page twenty?

This gallery had done a show a few years back, on abstraction and the environment. I clicked through the images of the show, and from the opening night, until I came to an image of a woman in front of a triptych of paintings.

I felt my stomach drop as I looked at the woman in the photo, a smiling brunette who stood proudly in front of a colorful, vaguely Ab Ex painting. I did the math quickly in my head, sizing up her age from the photo and the year of the exhibit. If I was right – and that kicking feeling in my gut told me I was – then this Isabella Gray must have been the older sister of the person who I suddenly felt sure had killed Lark. After all, they looked completely identical. With a foreboding feeling, I froze, my hand still hovering the mouse over the photo in front of me. I started to shudder as I realized: I had just spent the morning in class with a murderer.

I raced to close down my computer, taking a picture of the screen on my phone first, then snapping the laptop shut and gathering my things. I dashed off a quick text to Arun asking whether he could find out someone's maiden easily, hoping I wouldn't sound too enigmatic. While I waited for him to reply, I realized there was one person on campus who might remember Isabella Gray and be able to confirm my suspicions. I only hoped Agnes would still be in her office.

I weaved through the perpetual gridlock outside, racing back across the street and into our department's building. I paused at the top of the stairs, trying not to double over as I gulped in air, fully aware that catching my breath from a one block sprint should probably not be so hard for a twenty-two-year-old. Especially one who, as luck would have it, had to occasionally race after (or away from) killers.

Somewhat more composed, I strode down the hall to the faculty offices. Agnes usually retired to her office after the last class of the day, to have a cup of tea and field any panicking students before they left for the day.

I froze in the doorway to the offices. At the back of the room, in a small lounge area created from two office cubicles, Agnes sat in a comfy armchair, her customary tea already in hand. I could hear Martina's voice coming from her own office, directly across from the lounge.

Agnes shifted in her chair, turning around at the sound of my shuffled entrance. Martina peered out of her office.

"Samantha," she snapped. "Of course. Join us." There was

no questioning the command in her voice, and I walked slowly to the back of the room, till I could see both her and Agnes clearly. I clocked Martina's hand on her desk as she shut the desk drawer, my mind flashing back to all those bottles of eye drops I had seen the other morning. Dry eyes, my ass. I didn't know how, but I suddenly felt certain that it was the poison that had killed Lark.

"Hi, ladies," I stammered. "How's it going?" I couldn't be sure how much Agnes knew, but I had to stop her from drinking that tea. I caught her eye, looking pointedly down at the teacup, then up again, giving what I hoped was a barely perceptible shake of my head. Agnes only gave me a sad smile in response.

"We were just catching up about old times," Martina replied. "Agnes here was asking after my family. Isn't that right, Agnes?" Agnes stayed silent, having apparently learned enough to know what I knew: Martina had killed Lark.

"But you probably already know all about that, don't you, Samantha?" Martina asked. I couldn't help but appreciate the way she had seamlessly switched to my full name, dropping my preferred nickname, like in cartoons where all it takes to signal someone is a villain is to give them a pair of dark glasses. "You and your questions. Your poking around. Don't think I didn't see you rummaging around the sculpture studios. Do you really think things like that can go on around here without my knowing it?"

I hesitated, torn between playing it safe and wanting to point out that she had only been here for a couple months, and in reality, it was probably Agnes who had the all-seeing eyes of the department. I kept my mouth shut, at least until the silence grew too unbearable.

"You have an older sister," I said, finally making eye contact with Martina.

"Had. She's nothing now," Martina spat.

"Oh, I'm so sorry," I stammered. "I had no idea she had passed away."

Martina rolled her eyes in response. "She's alive," she said with a shrug. "But she's a shadow of her former self. A shadow of what she could have been."

"Because Lark ruined her career," I filled in.

"Isabella could have been a star. Lark could never stand anyone who was a real threat, someone who would really compete with him." Agnes nodded in agreement with this sentiment, still looking sadly down at her tea.

"So he had to die," I said to Martina. Now that the truth was out there, I knew we had a limited time to get out of here safely. It was one thing to run out of a dangerous situation on my own, but I had no idea how to save someone else along with me. I slowly reached into my pocket, hoping to get to my phone and signal for help.

"Not so fast, Samantha," Martina snapped, coming over and roughly grabbing my arm, yanking my phone out of my hand and throwing it across the room. "Do you really think I'm that stupid?"

"No, of course not, Martina," I said, trying to look apologetic and not just panicked that my only chance for calling for help had just been literally thrown out. I could hear a video class starting through the wall, and knew that no amount of screaming for help would be heard. "It was actually a pretty genius way to do it. To kill Lark, I mean. With all of the fake evidence."

Martina smiled smugly. "Yes, I know you had a fun little scavenger hunt looking for that. It kept everyone nice and busy.

But more to the point, Lark deserved to die in a terrible mess. Just like the ones he caused in real life," Martina said, her chin set, daring us to contradict her.

"What exactly did he do to Isabella?" Agnes asked quietly.

Martina turned the full force of her fury toward Agnes.

"What did he do?" she repeated. "He had her blacklisted, that's what. Isabella couldn't get another teaching job anywhere, not even at some middle tier school in Boston, of all places," she said venomously. The dig at Boston stung more than I would've liked to admit. "Isabella was reduced to showing in community galleries. In shows that weren't even juried!"

I tried my best to put on a look that said, *I commiserate with you, no need to kill me and my favorite mentor too*, even if I did have the strong urge to roll my eyes at the vehemence with which Martina believed that her sister's fate was worse than death.

"So how did you do it?" I asked, hoping that like most arrogant sociopaths, in my experience, Martina would enjoy explaining how she had pulled one over on everyone. Or almost everyone.

"Lark had no idea who I was," she said. "Most people thought Isabella and I were twins, but that awful man couldn't even be bothered to remember what she looked like, not enough to realize that we were related. Once I could be sure he didn't remember us, the rest was easy." She paused as Agnes moved to put her tea down on the side table. "Drink up, Agnes," Martina snapped. "Can't let that go to waste." Martina only continued once she was satisfied with the small sip Agnes took, ignoring me as I winced at the sight of Agnes having to drink something that was obviously poisoned. I tried to tune back in to what

Martina was saying while I looked around the room, scanning for anything that could help get us out of here.

"All I had to do was offer Lark a drink after his talk. It never occurred to the poor guy that there might be consequences for his actions." Martina folded her arms over her chest, daring me to ask any more obvious questions.

"And what about the eye drops?" I asked, nodding towards her desk.

"Yes, it was stupid of me to ask you to get them that day. But I had no idea then about your … 'extracurricular' activities," Martina replied. "But for Lark? It was fitting. A man who showed no remorse in life deserved to die by fake tears."

I hated to admit it, given the circumstances, but even I found it hard to disagree with her there. It did have a certain poetic justice to it. Or artistic justice.

"But now, Samantha, I think we've had enough questions," Martina said, moving back to her desk and the tea kettle that was still plugged in. I watched as she mixed me a drink, sensing that this was my only opportunity to get us both out of her safely.

Martina crossed the room back to me, holding out the drink. "Drink up!" she commanded. I took the mug, bringing it to my mouth in a pantomime of drinking, then flinging its hot contents out at her.

I leapt across the room, grabbing Agnes by the arm, tossing her tea behind us for good measure, even though Martina was still screaming at the back of the room. I ran for the hallway and the stairs down to the lobby, trying not to pull Agnes too roughly behind me. Although I shouldn't have worried – she was in better shape than I was, not even pausing to catch her breath as we tumbled toward the security desk at the door. I waved at Diego, still on duty, as if I were flagging down a cab and not signaling for help. I really needed to put some work into my emergency hand gestures.

"Martina!" I gasped, as Agnes more calmly and clearly laid out what was happening.

"I'm sure you guys are overreacting," Diego started, his hands firmly on his hips, even as I gestured wildly for him to pick up the phone and call for help. We all turned at the sight of Martina stalking down the stairs, her face a bright, scalded red, which only served to highlight her rage.

"Okay, yeah. That might be an emergency," Diego admitted, already dialing for the police. I pushed Agnes behind me, trying to stand up confidently as Martina made her way toward us, bracing myself for some kind of encounter. But luckily, there would be no need. We were surrounded by flashing lights before Diego even hung up the phone.

Chapter 19

A few weeks later, I regretted not yet finding the time to work on my cardio as I sprinted the last few blocks to school. I was clutching a plastic bag filled with water bottles in one hand, my other holding a newspaper over my head to block as much of the rain as I could. Which wasn't very much, as I could already feel my curls being pinned down by errant drops. I winced as I pictured the photo on the front page starting to bleed in the rain, the image under Arun's headline: ARTIST ARRESTED IN CRIME OF ARTISTIC PASSION. After giving me a strongly worded talking to about not running after murderers, calling for the police before I "really" needed it, etc., he had got right down to work, pulling several all-nighters to finish telling the story of Martina and Lark. Luckily for both myself and Detective O'Connor, Arun decided to leave me (mostly) out of it.

I stopped at a red light, the water bottles knocking heavily into my leg. The schedule having already been set, we were in the midst of our third visiting artist visit of the semester. Although some people had wanted to pause the program altogether, Agnes insisted that the entire community not be punished because of the misdeeds of one person. Of course, if you were the person tasked with running out in the rain to purchase the one particular brand of water said visiting artist would drink, it was hard to feel like you weren't still being punished.

On the other hand, whether we would admit it or not while we were busy talking trash about each artist, comparing each one's works and whims, picking out each tiny fault, this was what we all really wanted, hopefully in the not-too-distant future. Of course, without the murder part. Hopefully. Probably. Unless, you know, something happened and it was impossible not to get involved. I rolled my eyes in response as I imagined the look Arun would be giving me right now, and continued running back to school as fast as I could.

About the Author

Sarah Vernon is an author and artist based in Massachusetts, where she writes the Triple-Decker Mystery Series. You can find out more at www.vernonmysteries.com.

www.ingramcontent.com/pod-product-compliance
Lightning Source LLC
Chambersburg PA
CBHW020041310726
48970CB00007B/2357